C000059982

TH VOW

A BLACK ARROWHEAD NOVEL

USA TODAY BESTSELLING AUTHOR

DANNIKA DARK

All Rights Reserved
Copyright © 2020 Dannika Dark
First Edition: 2020

First Print Edition
ISBN-13: 979-8-6769-8039-9

Formatting: Streetlight Graphics

No part of this book may be reproduced, distributed, transmitted in any form or
by any means, or stored in a database retrieval system without the prior written
permission of the author. You must not circulate this book in any format. Thank
you for respecting the rights of the author.

This is a work of fiction. Any resemblance of characters to actual persons, living
or dead, is purely coincidental.

Edited by Victory Editing and Red Adept. Cover design by Dannika Dark. All
stock purchased.

www.dannikadark.net
Fan page located on Facebook

Also By Dannika Dark:

THE MAGERI SERIES
Sterling
Twist
Impulse
Gravity
Shine
The Gift (Novella)

MAGERI WORLD
Risk

NOVELLAS
Closer

THE SEVEN SERIES
Seven Years
Six Months
Five Weeks
Four Days
Three Hours
Two Minutes
One Second
Winter Moon (Novella)

SEVEN WORLD
Charming

THE CROSSBREED SERIES
Keystone
Ravenheart
Deathtrap
Gaslight
Blackout

Nevermore
Moonstruck
Spellbound
Heartless

THE BLACK ARROWHEAD SERIES
The Vow

DEDICATION

This book is dedicated to all my Seven series fans. Thank you for faithfully loving those characters. I hope you have room in your heart for new characters on their own journey to love.

To those of you who are new to my books: if you want to start with the origin story for these characters, check out *Seven Years*. If you decide to read this book first, just note that it contains a few spoilers to that series. If you prefer not to read the Seven books first, you won't miss a beat. This is a new adventure that stands on its own, so enjoy the ride.

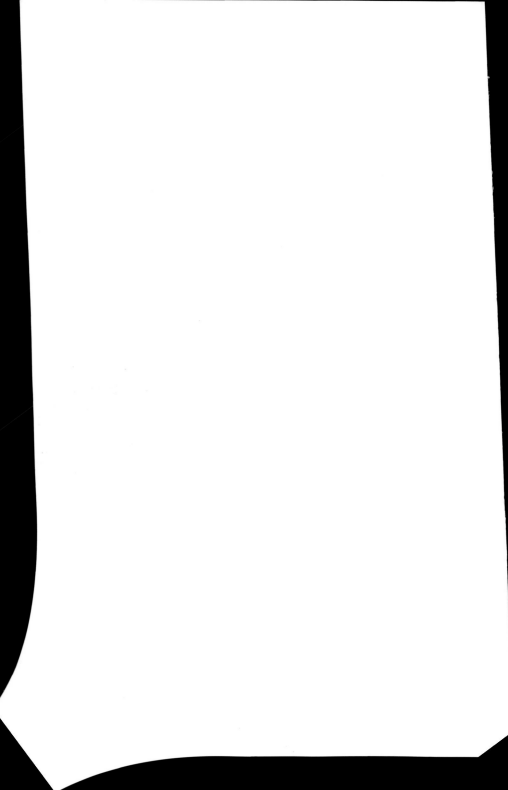

CHAPTER 1

I SAILED ACROSS THE EMPTY STORE, one knee on the seat of my rolling chair and my hands gripping the back. "We're business owners!" I exclaimed, unable to contain my excitement.

Opening my very own store had been a lifelong dream of mine since childhood. Well, not just mine but also Hope's. She was my best friend and soul sister. We'd begun our entrepreneurship years ago by selling our wares to kids in the local wolf packs.

Hope specialized in jewelry design. Most of it was fun and fashionable, but she also created beautiful, elaborate pieces that some folks were willing to pay a lot of money to own. I had a passion for fashion. My custom-made shoes, jackets, and other clothing had become so popular among our age group that even humans were asking where to buy them. But I only catered to Shifters. My former Packmaster had advised me against doing business with humans. Since the Breed world was kept secret, the less we interacted with humans, the better.

My chair slowed to a crawl in the middle of the shop, and I turned around to relax in it. Sunshine soaked into the wood floor, casting a magical spell that hung in the air like spun gold.

From her place on the floor, Hope tossed a dirty rag down and wiped her forehead with the back of her hand. "Well,

I'm done. I don't think the floor or the baseboards will get any cleaner. Whoever owned this place before us didn't do a good job keeping them clean. Bubble gum was stuck in all the corners." Strands of her long brown hair had pulled free from her ponytail, and she blew one away from her face.

"Do you think I should go over the windows once more?" I asked, noticing a few streaks that the sun had begun illuminating.

"Let it go, Mel. It took you hours to make them look this good, and you already fell off the ladder once." One of the suspenders on Hope's overalls slid off her shoulder, and she suddenly smiled, her brown eyes changing to the shape of crescent moons. "Remember when we used to pretend your brothers' fort was our store? We would decorate it and wait all day for customers. I'll never forget the time Hendrix and Lennon brought their friends over to play."

"And instead of yelling at us to get out, they wouldn't let their friends go home until they bought something. Poor kids." I smiled, remembering all the silly things we'd done growing up and how they had all led to this moment. "I told you this would happen. Your parents thought you would grow out of it and want to be a medicine woman."

She flashed a bright smile and drew up her knees. "It runs in the family, but I never had the desire. Maybe it's a nobler profession, but I love making things with my hands."

"Don't knock what we do. We're not saving lives, but maybe we're giving someone better self-esteem or putting a smile on their face, and that counts for something."

We each could have taken different paths in life to pursue other interests, as kids often did, but my brush with death in a freak snowstorm when I was seventeen had been the catalyst for making my dreams into a reality. I'd learned firsthand how unpredictable and fleeting life could be. So we'd made plans. *Real* plans.

When I could no longer keep up with the orders, I searched the online Breed newspaper and discovered a group of Shifters local to the Austin area who were offering seamstress services. Since I was just an inexperienced kid in their eyes, I had to work harder for their trust. I'd arranged a meeting to present my designs and discuss my sales growth, and I had also asked to see samples of their work to judge the quality. After that, I drew up a contract and made them an offer. With labor off my hands, I suddenly had an inordinate amount of time to strategize.

Hope dusted off the bottoms of her feet. "It's a good thing we found something in the Breed district. It's worth every penny. I would have hated to worry about taxes and all those inspections. Plus I like doing something for our community."

"Well, it's not like we can keep the humans out," I reminded her.

"I don't dislike them," she said quickly, obviously remembering that I'd grown up with humans in my pack. "But sometimes it seems like we have so little of our own in this world. You know?"

Since we couldn't keep humans from shopping in our stores, it was imperative that we took measures to protect our secrecy. Shopkeepers received protection from the local higher authority, and since Hope and I were Shifters, we could call upon our local Council for assistance. They had given us private phone numbers should the human law or government show up asking questions. Their insiders scrubbed memories and erased records—anything to keep Breed a secret from humans.

With our store launch just around the corner, we were already facing our first crisis. Hope had recently severed her business relationship with a gemstone dealer after he doubled his prices when he got wind that we were opening a store. We'd prepaid for a final shipment that would last us through the quarter, but after that, we were on our own. He was certain we would come crawling back to him with our grand opening on the horizon, but Hope had other ideas. Since she was Native American, she decided it would be in our best interests to work exclusively with a Shifter tribe. Not only would it put money back into the community, but also, Hope said they were men of their word and we wouldn't have to worry about someone screwing us over. Luckily, we still had time to sort all that out.

Hope admired the space. "This room has great light. And we're fortunate to not have competition nearby."

"That's for sure," I said, slowly swiveling my chair in a circle. "Sandwiched between an ice cream shop and a bakery—we couldn't ask for a better location." When my chair came to a stop, I stared absently out the window. "I just don't want it to look like one of those snooty boutiques. We need window displays that'll attract everyone, no matter their age or social class. Some of our friends will follow us, but I want to pull in the older crowd too—especially with all your high-end jewelry."

We both briefly turned to look at the glass jewelry counter by the register.

Hope tapped her finger against her chin. "Should we separate the merchandise by age group to make it easier for them to find what they want?"

"Let's mix it up first and see how that goes. I'm afraid if we put the teens here and the adults there, it'll segregate our customers and make the inventory appear limited. I get orders from grown women for my sneakers."

"You're right." Hope stood up and hooked her thumbs behind the straps of her overalls. She had thick eyebrows and never plucked them, which made her eyes look wild and beautiful, but she never played up her features with makeup. When she frowned, a tiny vertical crease appeared between her eyebrows. "Maybe we can dress the mannequins by age to show that we cater to both."

"That's a good idea." I twirled my violet hair around one finger and caught a whiff of the cleaning products still on my hands. "I'm so glad we did this on our own."

Hope lifted her can of soda and gracefully strolled forward.

She had a regal way about her that was natural and effortless. "Well, my *father* was certainly willing to help," she said with disdain. "You have no idea how close he was to buying this store for us—without our permission. He was insistent on us keeping the money we'd saved as a safety net."

"In case we fail?" I laughed and straddled the armless chair. When I noticed a loose thread hanging from my cutoff jean shorts, I yanked it off. "Our families mean well, but I don't want to be in their debt. If they had bought this place, it wouldn't feel like ours. They'd want to access our financial records and might even influence our decisions since they'd have a stake in the business. No, thanks. Where's our sense of accomplishment and independence? I'd rather fail on my own than succeed with someone else's money."

Hope chuckled and stood before me. "Is Wheeler still going to help?"

My uncle was a whiz when it came to financial advice—it was his calling in life. "That's a given. I trust him, and he's the one who combed through all that paperwork when we bought this place from the higher authority. If it weren't for him, we'd be situated two blocks over, by the antiques store."

"What was wrong with that place? It was bigger."

"Watching my aunt run her shop taught me how important foot traffic is, and the Vampires who hang around that street aren't exactly our target demographic. They're from the Old World and wouldn't be caught dead in my sneakers. We're better off near families—especially Shifters who like supporting one of their own." I pointed left and right. "Ice cream shop. Bakery. Boom, boom."

Hope smiled, her brown eyes sparkling. She tucked her hands in her pockets and worried her lip. "I'm scared."

So was I. In fact, I was terrified. I had nightmares of no one showing up on opening day. *What if Hope makes a killing with her jewelry and no one wants anything to do with my clothing line?* I would have no choice but to relinquish my half of the store so she could sell more merchandise. I'd considered that scenario as a real possibility, and as much as it would hurt, I had no problem giving it all to Hope. Better to support someone else's dream than to drag them down chasing your own. Egos don't pay the bills.

I glanced at the walls. "They did a good job with the paint."

She snickered at the cream-colored walls. "You have energetic brothers who are eager to please their sister. Did you see them racing each other?"

Rolling my eyes, I stood up. "That's why I had to yell at them to stop. I thought we'd end up with paint on the floors and the ceiling. Hendrix and Lennon are grown men. They should know better than to egg each other on."

"Grown men," she murmured. "You're older than them and still a baby yourself."

"Baby?" I strutted toward the counter, my chin held high. "I'm a twenty-five-year-old businesswoman."

She breezed by me. "Who rides around town on a red scooter. Why don't you get the grown-up kind that comes with an engine and doors?"

I rested my arms on the counter. "It's good exercise."

As she rounded the counter, she arched an eyebrow. "Are you sure that's the only reason? You have a lot of tails wagging every time you go flying by that bar on the corner. A lot of wolves have their eye on you for a mate."

"I don't think mating is what they have in mind, unless you mean in the bedroom. Guys don't get serious with girls like me. It's *you* they're lined up for."

She rested her chin in the palm of her hand. "Only because my father's one of the most powerful Packmasters in the territory and my mother is an influential figure in the community. She's the kind of woman every man wants to mate, but I am not my mother."

I understood where Hope was coming from. "Think about how *I* feel. My dad's a famous rock star, and my mom's gorgeous, outgoing, funny, and amazing."

"And you're not?"

I shrugged. "Well, I have my moments. But you know how it is. They're always comparing us to our parents and holding us to those standards, for good or for bad. Folks automatically assume I'm either a great musician or a drug addict."

Hope shook her head. "People should let go of the past. That's not the man your father is today."

"You're preaching to the choir. But I get all the good *and* the bad comparisons. I just want people to know me as that talented lady who owns the shop on Starlight Road."

Hope lifted her can. "I'll drink to that."

When the front door opened, we both turned to look. A man breezed through the doorway, his attention fixed on an electronic device. "Is either of you Hope Church or Melody Cole?"

Hope crossed the empty room to greet him. "I'm Ms. Church."

He scanned a small package on his device and handed it over. "Have a nice day."

After he tipped his cap and left the shop, I skipped toward her. "Our first mail! Who's it from?"

"It doesn't say."

As she tore away the brown paper, I handed her a miniature blade from my key chain to slice open the tape. Hope cradled the package in her left arm and let the bubble wrap fall to the floor. She pulled out a hand-carved wolf and turned it around.

I reached into the box to retrieve a folded piece of paper and read it aloud.

Dear Sister,

Congratulations on your store. I wish I could be there to celebrate your grand opening, but no worries. We'll see each other soon. I'm sending a wolf totem as a protector, so keep him by the

*register. Call me if you need anything, and tell
Freckles to break a leg.*

Lakota

Glancing at the phone number scribbled at the bottom, I
asked, "Who's Freckles?"

"Oh." Her cheeks bloomed red.

I dropped my arms to my sides. "Don't tell me. *I'm*
Freckles?" I walked to the counter and set the note down.

"It's just something between us that he started years ago
when asking about you. Don't be offended—you know he's
just being silly."

Silly was one word to describe her older half brother. Not
the adjective I would have chosen but fitting nonetheless. "It's
been years since I've seen Lakota. What's he up to?"

"Oh, about six feet."

"Seriously. You never talk about him anymore. Did
something happen?"

She bit her lip and set the wolf down. "Promise not to say
anything? It's a secret."

"He joined the circus, didn't he? I knew it." I snapped my
fingers for emphasis.

Playfully pushing my shoulder, she said, "Don't be silly."

"No, that's Lakota's job."

Hope circled her finger around the wolf's snout. The
carving stood eight inches tall, and the wolf looked like he was
guarding something. "He's been working as a bounty hunter."

I turned to face her. "Why's that a secret? Lots of Shifters
do bounty hunter work, especially alphas and betas. Two of
my uncles used to be bounty hunters."

"True," she said, her voice soft. "But have you ever asked
them about it? Most bounty hunters keep it a secret and only
tell close family members. We don't want to put him in any
more danger than he's already in. People gossip, and since
everyone knows our father, it's the kind of thing that would

spread fast in the wrong circles. Criminals like to know who all the active bounty hunters are, so it's best not to talk about it."

Thinking back, I realized we hadn't spoken about Lakota much. Whenever he would come up, Hope would always change the topic. Now I understood the stress she must have been going through—always worried that something awful could happen to her brother while she was unable to talk about it with anyone. Bounty hunting was dangerous work, but it paid well in both money and experience.

"Was it your choice not to tell me or his? I thought we were like family."

She frowned. "It's not that I don't trust you—"

"I'm not mad," I said quickly, not wanting to come across as a jerk. "If it was at your family's insistence, then I totally understand. But I just want you to know that you can trust me with anything—especially when it comes to family. We've known each other too long, and I don't gossip."

"I know that. You're a good friend, and maybe I was wrong for not saying anything. But you were also close to your pack."

She had me there. I loved my former pack and confided in them. Hope was probably afraid I might mention something to my mom or my aunt in a moment of weakness. And a couple of years ago, I might have. I'd never had anyone entrust me with something that big.

I looked down at the bracelet she'd given me long ago with Sister written on a metal plate.

Hope squeezed my hand. "Sometimes it's just easier not to burden someone with secrets. I wouldn't have wanted your family thinking you were keeping things from them. Not even my father's pack knows what he's doing—only family. They think he's still living up in Cognito with his adoptive parents. It's better this way until he makes enough money and connections to step away and do something else with his life."

"Don't worry. I won't tell a soul." My eyebrows arched as the truth began to sink in. "Who would have thought? Lakota

Cross, a bounty hunter. Time flies. I still remember a boy who used to play a lot of pranks."

"He's a man of thirty now, and we're proud of him. But sometimes we go long stretches without hearing from him. People put hits on bounty hunters, so my mother is hoping he'll be ready to join a pack soon. She worries so much for his safety. Lakota will make a strong second-in-command. He's building a reputation and a savings account that any decent Packmaster would respect." Hope glanced at the note again, her fingers tracing the numbers at the bottom. "His number changes a lot. He gives it to us in case there's an emergency, but we never call him. One call could put him in danger, so we wait for him to contact us."

"Sounds tough." I gave her a tight hug. "Now I feel like an insensitive ass for making jokes about him around you."

"You make me laugh, and sometimes I need the reminder that he'll be free of that life someday. I wouldn't have it any other way, Freckles."

Shaking my head, I pulled back. "Do me a favor and don't start calling me that."

She tamped down a smile. "He's never mentioned it to you?"

I patted the wolf sculpture on the head. "No. I guess if he has a pet name for me, I'll have to think of something really special for him so that the next time he comes to town—"

"No! Then he'll think I'm conspiring against him."

"Conspiring to do what?"

Hope grabbed the store keys. "To ruin his reputation. Lakota doesn't live around here, but respect is important to him. He'll kill me if you come up with an embarrassing nickname because you read his letter. Nicknames stick and not always in a good way. Promise me you won't do it?"

"Well, I guess it could be worse. He could have called me an eggplant." I tugged the ends of my hair.

"Don't be silly. That's an entirely different shade of purple."

I put my hands on my hips. "Why, Hope, are you being a smartass?"

"Guilty as charged." She pulled off her ponytail holder and shook out her tangled hair. "We have a long day tomorrow. Let's go home and order a pizza."

Tapping my finger on the wolf's nose, I said, "Guard the palace, boy."

Hope snickered and strode toward the door. "That gift was Lakota's way of telling every customer that we're Shifters."

"Why should that matter?"

Nearing the door, she glanced over her shoulder. "It's his way of warning people not to mess with us even though we're not in a pack. Wolves stick together."

CHAPTER 2

THREE SLICES OF PIZZA AND a bowl of mint ice cream later, I collapsed on our hot-pink sofa, magazine in hand. My hair was tousled and still damp from my shower, and I hadn't bothered to change out of my white terrycloth robe and blue slippers.

It was hard to believe that just one year ago, we were still living with our packs. Shifter children grow up knowing who and what they are, but most of the kids I knew didn't go through their first shift until their late teens or early twenties. After that, they left the pack as a rite of passage. Some mated right away, but most preferred to live on their own to prove their value in the community and sow those wild oats before joining a pack. A wolf wouldn't be considered a rogue at that age, not until they got older and openly resisted the idea of ever joining up with a pack. Hope and I hadn't moved until we'd adjusted to the whole shifting process. Cohabitation was essential for wolves, and we had to learn to control the shift and create a routine so our wolves could run.

The scary part about shifting was not remembering anything. Usually the alphas were the only ones who remembered the entire shift, but that wasn't the golden rule. Some Shifters blacked out right away, and others could remember a few seconds or minutes into their shift. After that, everything goes dark. And thank God for that. I couldn't imagine trying to share headspace with my animal spirit. Sharing a body was excitement enough. Not to mention introducing our wolves to the pack. When Hope and I decided to move in together, our Packmasters facilitated a meeting between our wolves.

They got along famously.

Not long after, we found a cute little apartment in the Breed district. Since most of the people on our floor were Shifters, we didn't have to worry about someone calling the cops because our wolves were howling. Once a week, when my wolf needed to run, I would go back home and shift on the property. My family lived only thirty minutes away, and they loved having me around. Sometimes my uncle Denver let his wolf run with mine. They were no longer my pack, but they would always be my family.

I glanced around at our grey walls, white crown molding, and eclectic artwork. We had fantastic space. The floor-to-ceiling windows on my left stretched all the way to the kitchen. A short pony wall ran from the left side to the end of the kitchen island. It seemed like a useless feature to divide the rooms since you could see over it, so Hope had set all her plants along the ledge.

The hot-pink couch was the centerpiece of the room—all the other furniture was a muted grey to match the walls. Pink accents throughout the room added pops of color, including a throw pillow, the painting behind me, and a vase on the corner table. The living room reflected my colorful personality—levelheaded with a dash of crazy. The kitchen on the far side of the room was all Hope, with its earthy color scheme and inviting atmosphere.

The front door suddenly opened. Hope tossed her keys on a small table, slammed the door, and darted down the hallway, which was on her immediate left.

"Everything okay with your mom?" I yelled. "There's still a bunch of pizza left over. Do you want me to heat it up?"

No reply.

A few minutes and a toilet flush later, she emerged from

the hall at a sluggish pace, having changed into a pair of sapphire-blue harem pants. Hope gravitated toward styles with a baggy crotch or a flared leg—anything that screamed comfort and obscured her feminine curves.

She plopped down on the sofa across from me and stared vacantly at the white coffee table between us. "Mel, I'm in real trouble."

"Did you break the toilet again?"

When she didn't smile, I sat up.

Hope tucked her hair behind her ears, her eyes downcast. "My supplier canceled the last shipment and refunded my money."

I blinked in surprise. "He can't do that! We've got over a hundred preorders and a store opening."

"Apparently he can." She sank back and drew her knees to her chest. "He wanted to double the price. I asked around, and because we didn't have a contract, he's within his rights. If I don't secure a new supplier and get a shipment within a week, we're toast."

A cold feeling of dread washed over me. I stared through the window at the night sky, struggling to make sense of how someone could be such an unprofessional asshole. "We'll just reach out to our customers. I'm sure they'll understand."

She threw her head back. "I've had time to think about this. We can't afford to lose customers with bad first impressions. Our reputation is on the line, and you know how the packs talk. Some of them are dying to see us fail, just because their packs don't get along with our former Packmasters."

I launched to my feet and waved my arm. "Well, screw them if they can't stand to see two women doing what they wished they could have done fifty years ago! I'm not about to be penalized for being ambitious. Some packs still sell moonshine for a living, and they want to judge us? The mind boggles."

She attempted a smile but failed dismally. Her pensive expression reminded me so much of her father. We came from different backgrounds, and because of that, we worked well as a team. Hope was reserved and planned everything, whereas I was the risk-taker who made impulsive decisions. My father had once said I was a Van Morrison song—a free spirit who didn't look before she leaped. Hope helped me look, and I helped her leap.

I sighed and folded my arms. "So what's the backup plan?"

Her eyes remained closed. "That final shipment would have lasted me another six months, but now... I don't know." She pressed the heel of her hand against her forehead. "I have three potential dealers."

"That's great news!"

She rolled her head to look at me. "Tribes don't negotiate over the phone. There's no way I can meet with all three of them and still help with the store opening. Two of them are close, but the third one—he's the most notable dealer in the country. Not many Shifter tribes deal in gemstones and precious metals. All the tribes respect him. The catch is he lives in Oklahoma."

"Why's that a problem? It's not that far of a drive."

"When I consulted my mother for advice earlier, she forbade me from going to Oklahoma."

I sputtered with laughter. "Forbade? Are you kidding?"

Hope lifted her head. "My estranged grandfather lives there, and she doesn't want me anywhere near his territory. I'm unclaimed by a pack, and she warned me that some of the packs up there are savages who take whatever they want. It's not worth the risk."

"Is the dealer in Oklahoma part of a pack, or is he a rogue?" I rounded the coffee table and switched on a lamp.

"Does it matter? He's one of the best, Mel."

"Just go. Maybe he's not even a wolf. The only way we'll earn the respect of people in this community is by standing on our own two feet."

Hope put her feet on the ground and leaned forward.

"*Dang it.* I know you're right, but I made a promise, and I keep my promises."

I strode toward her and sat on the coffee table. "Then *I'll* go. You interview the other two prospects, and I'll drive up to Oklahoma and work my magic. We can call each other and compare notes. You can make me a list of questions if there's anything you want me to ask him. I've worked with you long enough that I know what you're looking for and how to negotiate a deal."

Her eyes glittered with tears. "You would do that? What will your parents say about you going off alone?"

I laughed and leaned back. "My parents are the most liberal people I know. Now that we're on our own, we don't answer to a Packmaster. It's hard to get used to, but we don't require anyone's permission. That'll change if we ever join a pack, but let's make the most of it. You made a promise, and because of the whole family thing, I get it. But no one from my old pack is going to bat an eyelash. I've gone up there a few times on hunting trips, plus it's only for a day or two."

She clasped my hands in hers. "Everything's going to work out. It has to! Can you believe we're going to open our own boutique? A store called Moonglow, and we're located on Starlight Road. That's a good sign. The fates are watching over us."

"Of course they are. We're fashionista rock stars. Not everyone's cut out to be a moonshine dealer."

We laughed long and hard, laughter you can only share with your best friend. The kind that ends in tears, cramped stomachs, and embarrassing snorts. The kind that measures a friendship, reminding you just how unbreakable that bond really is.

Time was of the essence, and we were in survival mode. Hope had spoken with all three dealers on the phone and scheduled meetings, but that meant losing time needed to prepare for our grand opening. Somehow we had to race out of town, secure a deal, and haul ass to get back and set up the store.

The first thing we did was figure out transportation. Since Hope had to drive to San Antonio first then back up to Waco, I told her to keep the car we shared. That worked out for the best because borrowing one from her old pack would only raise questions, and we didn't need the added stress of Lorenzo Church sticking his nose in our business. He was extremely protective of his daughter, and that would never change, whether she was twenty-four or six hundred. That was just the way alphas were. It was easier for me to borrow a car from my family without receiving the third degree.

When the doorbell rang, I finished changing into my pajamas and dashed down the hallway toward the front door. "Coming!"

Hope flattened her back against the wall as I rushed past her into the living room.

Out of breath, I swung the door open and looked up at a tall man with large brown curls. Uncle Will had the kind of messy hair that women swooned over, not that he ever noticed.

He held a set of keys between two fingers and jingled them. "May I ask what this clandestine meeting is about?"

I snatched the keys and stepped back to let him in. "Can I get you something to drink?"

The door closed behind him. "I would love some absinthe."

"I see your sense of humor is still intact." After padding into the kitchen, I pulled a bottle of root beer from the fridge. "Thanks for coming on short notice. Sorry to be all secretive about borrowing your car, but take a seat, and I'll explain. And don't worry about paying for a cab to get home. That's on me."

Will swaggered over to our large kitchen island and sat down. After setting the bottle in front of him, I switched on the mosaic pendant lights, the soft glow from the three bulbs illuminating the granite countertop.

"How's the family?" I asked, taking a seat across from him.

He popped the lid off his bottle, and a small cloud of moisture hovered on the rim. "Eager to attend your grand opening."

"Well, they don't have to come if they don't want to. I mean, I'd love for them to come, but if they're busy—"

"We're coming. Do you think we would miss the most important day of your life? You seem more nervous than usual. Mustn't worry. It'll be fine."

"It's nerve-racking when it's your own shop."

He pushed his bottle forward and folded his arms on the counter. *Uh-oh.* I could sense the serious talk coming.

"Mel, you know I counsel packs. It's what I do. Not just with Packmasters, but I help people create goals and work out problems. I want to take off my uncle hat for a minute. Anytime you need to talk privately to someone, my door is open. Whatever we talk about will remain confidential, just as it is with my paid clients. Moving out of a pack is a tough transition, but it's an important test of one's strength. The yearning to belong never diminishes. I've seen young women make decisions in haste—mating with men they didn't love in order to be part of a pack again."

I chuckled softly. "You don't have to worry about that. I quit dating two years ago."

Tension filled the room, and he furrowed his brow. "Did something happen?"

"No, it's nothing like that." I was hesitant about laying it all out.

He sensed my reluctance and eased forward with those kind eyes of his. "I won't judge you."

I peered around him to make sure Hope wasn't in the room. "I grew up with two parents who have the most explosive chemistry on the planet. What's the point of going through the motions of relationshipping when I don't feel a fraction of that chemistry with any of the men I date? My parents set the bar unrealistically high, and I have serious doubts that there's anyone out there who could make me feel that loved. Anyhow, I have too much going on with the business. Or maybe I'll put off dating until I'm a hundred."

He pursed his lips and studied me for a moment. "You won't be able to resist the pull toward pack life for long. There's no reason to rush into dating, but keep in mind that it's better for you to join a pack through mating. It gets... complicated when single Shifters enter a pack."

My uncle was right. Sometimes it worked out, but I'd heard stories over the years about new packmates causing a stir. A woman entering without a mate would catch the eye of more than one single man in the house, disrupting the harmony within the pack, and the same might apply with gender roles reversed. The idea of an unplanned pregnancy was terrifying. *Without a mate, who will keep me from humping the first available man when I go into heat?* At least with Hope around, I had someone to make sure I didn't leave my room and do something stupid during those days. *What if the pack I choose doesn't have a heat house or separate facility for me to stay in during my time of need? What if I have one of those single Packmasters who decides it's his job to slide my panties down and give me orgasms without sex to shorten the duration? How weird would that be if I didn't even like him?* I shuddered.

"The idea of living with another pack is terrifying," I admitted.

He laced his fingers together. "So is being a lone wolf. Eventually the need to bond with a family will become overwhelming. Keep your heart open to possibilities. There's no need to rush into mating, but don't close the door either. You could wind up shutting out your soul mate." Will sat back and relaxed his shoulders. "Just remember that I'm here when you need to talk. It's good that you and Hope have each other to lean on. But if she mates with someone first, you'll be left alone."

I hadn't thought about that. My chest tightened at the idea of losing Hope to a mate. When young wolves moved out of packs, it was common for them to live in groups—especially women—until they mated or found a pack of their own. I didn't have anyone else except my brothers, and I didn't want to live with them.

"Thanks, Uncle Will. My parents gave me advice since they both lived alone for a long time. Probably too long. It might not seem like it, but I really love my independence. Just don't get the wrong idea if I come home a lot for dinner. It doesn't mean I want to move back in. I just miss it. You know?"

"Indeed." He reached out and placed his hand on mine—a consoling touch that I needed more than I realized. "We're proud of you, Mel. It's not easy being an assertive female in business affairs. Just ask the women in our pack. It intimidates a lot of men in the community who don't strive as hard. If anyone threatens you, let us know. We'll always have your back."

My eyes darted away.

"What's wrong?" He leaned in tight, and it made the hair on the back of my neck stand up. Male Shifters possessed a palpable energy when provoked or in protective mode, and he missed nothing.

I withdrew my hand. "Someone wrote on our window with shoe polish."

That was why I'd spent all my afternoon scrubbing those windows. It offended me to know that someone had targeted us, and I didn't want a single trace of it left behind.

"What did it say?"

My cheeks heated. "Slut."

His jaw clenched, and he sat back. Will usually kept his cool and wasn't one of the aggressive wolves in the pack. Only twice had I ever seen him lose his temper, and it wasn't a pretty sight.

Before he could say anything, I continued. "We can't put cameras up since security cameras aren't allowed in the Breed district, especially outside. It's probably kids or maybe even some jealous competition. Anyhow, we're wolves, and wolves stand their ground. The writing washed off, and we're not dwelling on the matter. Aunt Lexi told me she had some trouble with her bakery in the beginning, but people got over it."

He scraped his teeth against his bottom lip. "She was also mated to a Packmaster. People see you as an easy target—someone they can push around since you're unclaimed."

"And that's why I don't want to mention this to the pack," I said, holding his gaze. "You don't have legal rights to take action against someone who's harassing me since I don't belong to the pack anymore. The last thing I want is retaliation. I love my family but not enough to see you go to Breed jail over a few dumb rednecks who are intimidated by a couple of women."

Will gave a handsome smile, erasing his dark expression. "You make a fair argument, but you mustn't keep secrets from us. If there's no one you trust in the pack, then speak with me. I have connections, and if you receive continued harassment, then maybe we can figure something out. You know all about the bidding war with real estate. A lot of packs want commercial property, so that's why they're hoping that you fail or give up. You won this property over a long list of people, so don't be surprised by a little backlash in the community. They'll get over it."

I straightened my back. "I don't give up. Never have, never will. And I promise to tell you if we run into trouble again. That's been the only incident. Hopefully the last."

Hope approached the kitchen island, clasping her hands. "Hi, William."

Will turned in his seat and stood, arms wide. "How's my girl?" He gave her a quick hug and looked between us. "Have you been watching over our Mel and keeping her out of trouble?"

Amusement danced in her eyes as she folded her arms. "She's in capable hands."

"Of that I have no doubt." He glanced down at her bag near the door, his eyes brimming with concern. "I think it's time that you tell me why I'm here. Are you two going somewhere?"

Her eyes darted toward me, and I stood up.

"That's why I need to borrow your Jeep," I confessed. "We ran into a last-minute snag with one of our contractors, so we're on borrowed time to find a new one as quickly as possible. We have separate meetings set up tomorrow, and Hope's taking the car. My scooter isn't going to get me very far on the highway."

"Do you need someone to escort you?"

"No," I blurted, sensing that protectiveness kicking in. "And please don't mention this to Lennon or Hendrix. You know how they are, and they'll follow me. I don't need two macho alphas flanking me at all times and intimidating the hell out of everyone. What if they insult the dealer and ruin our chances? The thing is, no one is going to take me seriously if I show up with a male escort."

Hope erupted with laughter.

"That sounded all wrong," I said, shaking my head. "What I meant was—"

"No need to explain." His lips twitched before he nodded in agreement. "They'll assume you can't make decisions on your own. If this person is a Shifter, he'll have more confidence striking a deal if you negotiate alone."

I leaned on the counter. "Showing up with my brothers just isn't professional."

William turned away in a pathetic attempt to conceal his grin. It didn't take a detective to figure out what had him so tickled. I had to laugh at the thought of me rolling up in a flashy red Jeep, my purple hair flying everywhere. The guy was going to take one look at me in my eccentric clothes and think I'd escaped the circus.

Which was exactly what my life had become.

CHAPTER 3

"H OW'S THE DRIVE?" HOPE ASKED on my speakerphone.

I glanced at the mess of candy wrappers on the passenger seat of my uncle's Jeep. "Scenic. And if one more trucker wags his tongue between two fingers at me, I'm going to drive off a cliff."

She laughed. "Let me know when you see a cliff in Texas."

"As a matter of fact, I'm already in Oklahoma. I'm sure if I look hard enough, I can find one. If not, the noxious odor of dead skunks every thirty miles should do me in. Where are you?"

"I just left."

Turning down the air so I could hear better, I said, "Wait a second. Weren't you going to leave right after me?"

"I wish I had. It took me over an hour to find a decent hotel online."

I passed a pickup truck and grinned. Hope was a planner and didn't like the idea of staying at the first motel on the side of the highway. When I'd left the apartment, she was on the internet, comparing amenities.

"Traffic is a nightmare," she continued, "so it's probably going to take me a couple of hours before I make it to San Antonio."

I glanced down at the clock. "How long do you think your meeting will last?"

"It depends. We're having dinner at the hotel, and if that goes well, he'll probably invite me back to his place."

"Sounds kinky."

When her response came through garbled, I moved the phone around. "Hope?"

"I'm here. And don't be silly. His elders want to speak with me. The tribes are careful about who they do business with, so he's basically vetting me to see if I'm good enough to consider."

"Well, just watch out for yourself. He might be one of those crazy alphas with a harem."

"I'm glad I packed my harem pants."

Chortling, I said, "I really shouldn't laugh at that."

"I'm more worried about you. It's not too late to turn back."

I jerked the wheel and swerved around roadkill. Thankfully it wasn't a skunk. "Don't worry about me. I brought my bow and arrows. The only thing I forgot to pack was some good music. Uncle Will's fantabulous CD collection leaves *much* to be desired."

"It can't be that bad."

I picked up a jewel case and read the label. "Let's just say that when I lost the radio stations, I was reduced to listening to Herb Alpert and Engelbert Humperdinck."

"Who?"

"Exactly. These are the joys of living with old Shifters. Do you think one day our kids will be laughing at our music?"

The reception cut off, and I only heard every other word.

"Hope? I'm going to let you go before I drop off. Call me later."

"Okay. Drive safely."

Another flash of lightning streaked across the dark horizon up ahead. It had been nothing but blue skies until I hit Dallas. As soon as I'd passed the casino in Oklahoma, the sky turned midnight blue, and headlights lit up the highway in both directions.

Now there *was* no highway, just miles and miles of trees along the two-lane road. I'd only seen two cars in the past thirty minutes, and there wasn't anywhere safe to pull over. Every so often, I passed a run-down home with dogs chained up in the front yard.

I reached for the map and flattened it against the steering wheel. *Where the heck does this guy live? What if he's a lion Shifter or some crazy rogue who lives in the woods and decorates his cabin with dead squirrels?* For all I knew, I might have been meeting with a Mage or a Vampire, and the thought of some guy sucking my blood or my energy for a high and leaving me on the side of the road left me with a sinking feeling.

Too late to turn back now.

"Good grief. Where's a gas station when you need one?"

I didn't have enough light to see the map, not without driving off the road.

"A sign would be helpful," I muttered. "I've passed two intersections with no signs. It's like they *want* you to get lost in this state. Welcome to Oklahoma." I made a sweeping gesture with my arm. "Stay. *Forever.*"

When "Spanish Eyes" came on, I turned down the volume. Fat drops of rain hammered against the car like wild applause.

"Uh-oh," I sang. "Please don't hail."

Uncle Will loved me, but that was likely to change if his Jeep came home resembling a golf ball with dents all over his beautiful red finish. Men loved their cars, and borrowing a man's car was like borrowing a child. If anything happened to it while in my care, even an act of God, I would never hear the end of it. Not that he would yell at me, but Uncle Will had a quiet way of getting his disappointment across that was far worse than verbal confrontation.

I reached another intersection and slowed to a stop. The cross street was marked Private Property on both sides, but to the left were several taillights flashing in the distance. The

the bees and the wolves. Bending over or showing my back to a Shifter had a meaningful connotation among adults—one that was part of the dance when seeking out a mate.

I pivoted on my heel and lingered by the jukebox before settling on a stool near the end of the bar. Through the mirror behind the bottles, I noticed eyes swinging away as the men lost interest.

"What can I get you?" the bartender asked.

I set my purse on the bar along with the map. "I'm famished. I'll have the burger and fries. No pink meat."

He had a peculiar grin, showing more of his bottom teeth than his top ones. "What to drink?"

"Root beer."

"Did she say root beer?" a man barked. A few cackles sounded from that direction.

I glared at the man sitting three stools down while unfolding my map. Hope had warned me that the rural areas had pockets of Shifters who were lawless and uncivilized. They considered most outsiders interlopers and treated them accordingly.

The bartender spoke quietly with him, and their direct stares bored a hole into my skull. When he returned with my root beer and popped the lid, someone snickered. Ignoring them, I sent Hope a text.

> **Melody**: I'm in hell.
>
> **Hope**: I thought you were in Oklahoma.
>
> **Melody**: It's raining. Had to pull over.
>
> **Hope**: Where?
>
> **Melody**: A tiny bar in no-man's-land. The roads here are confusing.
>
> **Hope**: You must be in Shifter territory. They're not all marked. You okay?

Melody: Just wish you were here. Reception is iffy, so don't panic if I go quiet for a while.

Hope: Maybe you'll meet Mr. Right.

Melody: More like the missing link. Talk soon.

I smiled and put my phone away. While I squeezed the ends of my wet hair and listened to Hank Williams Jr. growling on the jukebox, I noticed something peculiar. There weren't any women. I didn't recall seeing any on the other side of the wall, either. And I found that odd.

As much as I wanted to turn around and make sure I wasn't imagining things, the last thing I wanted to do was give anyone the impression that I was checking them out. Men often outnumbered women in Shifter communities. That wasn't the strange part. But guys, especially alphas, loved having their women by their sides. Even Shifters who lived in mansions liked to get out and socialize, including women. Perhaps I'd wandered into the Bermuda Triangle of the South.

Just as I found my location on the map, my burger magically appeared.

"Ketchup?" the bartender asked.

"No, thanks," I said warily, eyeing my smashed bun. "Can I have some mustard?"

"There's a gas station five miles up the road. Ketchup is all we've got." He patted the bar twice. "I'm Red. If you need anything, just holler."

My uncle Denver worked as a bartender, and if I knew one thing, it was how long it took to properly grill a burger. This wasn't fresh. It was a precooked patty he'd tossed in the microwave. The bun had that distinct freezer burn smell bread gets when it's been in cryosleep for too long and is then revived in a toaster oven.

"Is the city girl too good for our food?"

I swung my eyes to the man sitting three stools over— the one with a grizzly bear tattooed on his forearm and a camouflage cowboy hat atop his head. "Is the country boy too good for manners?"

The two men on either side of him heckled him. "She got you there, Jimmy."

When the jukebox switched over to Patsy Cline, I resumed squinting at the map. Shikoba, the dealer I was meeting with, had provided directions that began with street names and ended with landmarks. "Turn right when you see a big rock" and "turn left at the white tree." The rain needed to let up so I could *see* the big rock and the white tree.

"Something wrong with your burger?" Red asked.

When I heard the disappointment in his voice, I took a bite. No sense in insulting the staff. It required all the strength I could summon to swallow that bite, and I struggled not to gag when I realized it wasn't beef. Probably deer meat, or maybe something else was added as filler. I quickly shoved a handful of fries into my mouth and washed it down with root beer. "Do you know where I can find a man named Shikoba?"

He rested his forearms on the bar, and I spied a grease stain on his button-up denim shirt. "Are you law?"

"No. Just a friend."

Jimmy leaned over the bar to grab a stack of napkins. "You're friends with an injun?"

"Quiet down," Red snapped.

Oh, what redneck hell did I just walk into?

I'd visited Oklahoma several times, and usually the locals were amiable people. Then again, I'd never been around these parts. Regardless of the flagrant use of offensive words, I had a job to do, and someone in here might be able to point me in the right direction so I could be on my merry way.

Red leaned in and said quietly, "Don't mind him. He recently lost his mate and ain't been himself."

"Do you know anyone by that name?" I asked Red.

Jimmy leaned forward and pushed up his camo hat with his index finger. "They all sound the same to me. Like someone hacking up a lung."

My blood boiled. Thank the fates Hope hadn't come with me, or else I would have gotten my arrows out of the car and taught Jimmy some manners.

The thought was still playing out in my head while I methodically folded my map, making sure each crease was precise. "I just assumed you guys were local and knew everyone around here. My mistake."

Someone circled around to my right, slowly, so I would feel his presence as he appraised me. When the black-haired man spoke, it was edged with humor. "Twenty dollars says she's a bobcat."

I smiled up at him. "I've got thirty riding on you being an asshole."

His eyebrows arched high. "Yep. She's lippy. Definitely a predator. Grizzly?"

Jimmy spoke gruffly. "She's *not* a grizzly."

The bartender laughed. "And how do you know that, Jimmy? She bathes?"

Then the power flickered, followed by a crash of thunder. Several men in the back hollered, clearly enjoying the light show outside.

I ate more fries, amused by the banter among the men. It wasn't uncommon for Shifters to have a little fun with the tourists by guessing their animal. It had become a recreational pastime, and my old pack had engaged in the same behavior numerous times back at Howlers on a slow night.

I whipped my head around when I heard a *baaaa*.

The bartender peered over the bar. "Will one of y'all get Freddy the hell out of here? Damn drunk. Hurry up before he shits on my floor."

Jimmy slid off his barstool and picked up the goat. "Come on, Freddy. You ain't supposed to be in here on the weekdays, anyhow."

And just when I thought things couldn't get any stranger…

A formidable man entered the bar. His brown hair, just past his shoulders, blew forward and tangled when a gust of wind carried in the strong smell of rain. Lightning flashed behind him, and he didn't so much as flinch at the thunderclap. He stood at the entrance as if he were guarding it, his blue eyes arresting.

Chills swept over my arms, and for the first time, I felt butterflies in my stomach. Not the kind you got when danger was imminent but something else entirely, something that made me suck in a breath and hold it.

Lakota Cross, Hope's older brother, had matured into a handsome man whose very presence commanded attention. It was as if he'd shed every last boyish feature he'd carried into his twenties. Now thirty, he possessed a magnetic aura—one that could easily be mistaken for an alpha wolf, even though he wasn't.

The white T-shirt beneath his leather jacket hugged his body. Not an ounce of fat was visible. I was so used to seeing him in sweatshirts or long shorts that it took me a second to soak it all in. He tucked his hands in his jeans pockets and fell into a staring contest with Jimmy, whose lip curled at the sight of him. Just as Jimmy exited the building, two Natives entered the bar and flanked Lakota.

They garnered stares from a few men sitting at the bar. It was in that moment that it occurred to me that all the men sitting in the booths on the other side of the divider wall were Native American, and none of the men on my side were. It was as if I'd stepped into a time machine and transported myself to 1952, and not in a good way.

I patted my hand against the bar to summon the bartender. "Exactly what are the rules in here?"

He popped open a bottle of beer before answering. "No fighting, no shifting, and no skipping out on the tab."

"That's it?"

When he pointed behind me, I glanced up at the wall over the jukebox to a sign I'd failed to notice. It was wooden, and the red paint had faded. An arrow pointed to the right, and the lettering read TRIBES.

Which meant the place segregated patrons. Two black men were doing shots at a booth behind me, so it had nothing to do with skin color and everything to do with the local tribes. I'd never seen anything like it in Austin. Some Shifters resented Natives because they owned good land passed down from their ancestors—land that neither the white settlers nor the higher authority had gotten their hands on. Usually I'd seen the animosity in the form of a few grumbles between packs, but nothing like this.

I swung my gaze to Lakota as he swaggered toward me, his eyes slicing across the room. As he closed the distance between us, my heart quickened. *Will he recognize me? What is he doing here?*

The moment his eyes slanted in my direction, my stomach tightened into a knot.

"Better keep those eyes in your head," a man at the bar spat. "Don't look at our women."

Now *these rednecks are coming to my defense?*

I could almost hear my heart beating with each step he took. *Thump. Thump. Thump.*

Recognition flickered in his eyes, and they widened just a fraction. When he averted his gaze and moved past me without a word, I realized I wasn't supposed to know him, and he wasn't supposed to know me. I sized up his two friends, each wearing a single braid down their back. They kept their eyes trained on the wall, uninterested in the dripping-wet woman who was gaping at them. I could smell rainwater on their clothes as they walked by and disappeared around the divider wall.

I faced forward and frowned at the bartender. "If you don't like them, why not ban them?"

The bartender laughed and shook his head. "I got nothing against the tribes. They're half my income. We got a bunch of old-timers living around here, though. The wall keeps everyone happy, and I don't have to break up as many fights. Ain't one of them complained about it."

I lifted my root beer and gave him a mirthless smile. "That's really progressive of you."

The black-haired man on my right turned toward me and drummed his fingers on the bar. "Where you from?" he asked, his voice threaded with suspicion. He didn't have the same twang as everyone else. His accent was a slow Southern drawl that told me he wasn't local.

"Texas."

He narrowed his eyes and smiled. "And your pack?"

"It's rude to ask what my animal is."

He scratched his five o'clock shadow. "I wasn't asking. I was… making an assumption. Bitches are so easy to spot."

Bitch wasn't a word in my former pack's vocabulary, but it was a common, innocuous term among Shifters. Despite his friendly banter, my head was still reeling from seeing Lakota. *What are the odds?*

It made sense that he was taking jobs where there were more tribes. He could easily blend into the fold. Having been raised in both cultures, Lakota would have no trouble relating to the nontribal outlaws as well.

But here, in the middle of nowhere? What kind of insidious crimes are happening at the corner of the white tree and the big rock?

Staring back at that sign was making my stomach roil. I'd always considered Hope's family an extension of mine. Their culture was steeped in tradition, and it had never been an "us and them" situation. Racism existed among Breed, but it was between different animals or Breed types, not because of color or heritage. No one trusted Vampires, Mages and Chitahs were mortal enemies, Shifters were looked down upon because of our past as slaves, and Sensors weren't taken seriously since their business practices were seen as perverse.

It made me ashamed to be sitting on the side I was, but something told me the resentment flowed both ways. The place had a history all its own that my brief visit and a few enlightening speeches weren't going to change.

Jimmy returned to his seat and tossed his camo hat on the bar. "Someone tell them to keep it down," he complained to the bartender. "A man can't think with all that hootin' and a-hollerin'."

The noise on the opposite side of the wall amplified—boisterous laughter overlapping the chatter. The bartender left his station and disappeared around the corner. Moments later, the volume dropped just as fast as turning a dial down on a radio. He returned, filled two pitchers of beer, and disappeared again.

Rubbing my finger against the condensation on my glass, I asked the dark-haired man beside me, "Where are all the women?"

He shrugged. "Not many single girls in these parts."

I chuckled. "So you keep them home, barefoot and pregnant?"

He cocked his head to the side. "Maybe a lady has no business being in a rowdy place like this."

I glanced at the décor and sipped my drink. "I can't say I blame them."

"Sometimes a mated one comes in for a drink… *without* her mate. That usually stirs the pot. Are you tied to anyone?"

Since I really wasn't in the mood for a personal interrogation about my love life, I kept stuffing cold fries into my mouth.

When he touched my hair, I drew back. "Hands off," I said. "This isn't a petting zoo."

"Sorry. I mistook you for a peacock with that color."

"Maybe you should buy a bottle for your mate."

"Maybe."

"A Shifter who's truly in love wouldn't be caught dead hitting on a stranger in a bar."

"She doesn't care what I do," he said matter-of-factly. "We have an open relationship, and I'm always open to taking in another mate."

While he rambled on, I couldn't shake the image of Lakota out of my mind. My thoughts drifted back to many years ago when I'd lost my way in a snowstorm. I'd walked in circles on our property, unable to see in the darkness. I was cold and frightened—my pride and confidence stripped away. Then I remembered how Lakota appeared out of nowhere, like a knight on horseback. It was the first time I'd ever felt my heart quicken. The fates had always put him in the right place when I needed him, so it made me apprehensive as to why we were having yet another chance meeting.

"So what do you think?" the man asked.

I blinked at him. "What?"

A humored grin stretched across his face. His aquiline nose and large nostrils made his features appear narrower than most. He tucked his fist against his chin. "You didn't hear a word I said, did you? What could be going on in that pretty little head of yours?"

"Maybe I was just coming up with solutions for the world's energy crisis."

A shadow appeared in the corner of my eye, and I peered over my shoulder. Lakota was facing the jukebox, his palms resting on the top as he leaned forward, shifting most of his weight to one leg. My gaze swung down to his ass, and normally I didn't notice such a thing on men, but Lakota had a noteworthy frame. He wasn't overly tall—just a few inches over me. I liked that. I'd always liked it when a man was closer to my level. It meant my face would fit perfectly in the crook of his neck.

Not that my face had spent much time in the crook of any man's neck recently.

I couldn't strip my eyes away from him. He was my best friend's brother, and I had absolutely *no* business memorizing his ass.

Lakota slowly pushed a button, and the energy in the room fired up to the beat of "Cradle of Love" by Billy Idol.

He casually glanced over his left shoulder and locked eyes with mine. In that moment, something transpired between us. My entire body flushed with embarrassment, as if he could somehow sense I'd been admiring him. He drank me in, down to my shoes and back up to my eyes. I couldn't see his mouth to tell if he was smiling, but his provocative gaze made my throat dry.

I jerked my head toward the mirror in front of me and took a swig of root beer. My hair was damp and tousled, my eyeliner smudged, and my tank top still wet. I casually swiped my finger beneath my eyes to fix my makeup, ignoring the fact that I could still feel him staring at me while Billy Idol screamed about teasing and pleasing.

It made me aware that I was straddling my stool more than sitting ladylike. He *had* to have recognized me, but I wondered what his impression was. The last time he'd seen me, I had blue hair. *Or was it pink?*

"You got a problem?" Jimmy growled. He was addressing Lakota.

My eyes fixed on the mirror when Lakota sauntered up. He eased between us and extended his arm, signaling the bartender for a beer with one finger. He smelled like leather and musk. It became incredibly difficult to remain nonchalant, especially with a guy who had always been playful with unrestrained physical affection.

The bartender popped the lid to a bottle and set it in front of him. When Lakota slowly turned toward me, he drew in a deep breath as if taking in my scent. His lips pressed tight like those of a man who wanted to say something. But he played it cool and strode off with his beer.

Jimmy lowered his voice. "You stay far away from them if you know what's good for you. Those redskins ain't nothing but murdering savages."

I clenched my jaw. *So help me, if someone uses a derogatory word one more time, I am going to set this place on fire.* The last thing I needed to do was lose my temper and accidentally shift, so I pulled out my phone as a form of distraction.

"I'm dead serious," he continued. "Some of the women

around here look at them like forbidden fruit. Well, you know what happens to people who eat forbidden fruit."

I looked at him with disdain. "They gain knowledge?"

"They get thrown out of the garden."

"Go back to your beer, Jimmy," the man to my right said, a smile playing on his lips. He propped his elbow on the bar so he was facing me all the way, his body language open. "I'm Crow."

"Is that your animal or what you like to eat?" I gave him a sardonic smile and gulped down my drink.

Crow wasn't my type. Imperious attitudes were common among Shifter men, especially when they were flirting, so that wasn't a deal breaker.

But the way he kept inviting himself to touch me *was*.

I brushed his hand away from my arm. "Maybe you should go check on your goat in the parking lot so I don't hit him with my car when I leave."

"Anything I can do to make you stick around for another drink?"

I swiveled to face him. Because my wet tank top had stretched lower than usual, his eyes took an unapologetic detour down to my cleavage. He looked slightly disappointed at my shortcomings. My breasts were large enough to identify me as a woman but did not hold a man's rapt attention for long. My legs, on the other hand, did.

But Crow never got that far. His gaze fixed on the turquoise pendant around my neck—one Hope had urged me to wear as a means to impress the dealer. "What was the name of the person you're looking for?"

"Shikoba. Do you know where he lives? I just want to make sure I'm heading in the right direction. And before you ask, my business is none of your business."

He lit up a cigarette and took a drag. "Look, normally I don't get mixed up in their affairs, and you shouldn't either, if you were smart. This isn't the big city, and naive little girls like you get hurt. But I'm a sucker for a damsel in distress."

When laughter broke out on the other side of the room, I recognized Lakota's laugh. Somehow, my brain filtered it from all the others. *What is he doing here?*

Crow released a smoky breath and gestured to my folded map. "Let me have a look at that."

I handed it over and watched him analyze it closely.

"Here," he said, pointing near two faded lines. "The turnoff is right past my place. It's easy to get lost in Running Horse. We're not on the map. Want me to show you the way?"

"No, that's not necessary. If I can navigate I-35, I can do anything. Thanks for the info." I hopped off my stool and dug through my purse.

"Don't I get a name? Or should I just call you Violet?"

"So we're here?" I asked, pointing at intersecting lines to confirm.

When I answered his question with a question, he stared at me for a spell. Finally, Crow shook his head and moved my finger to the left. "No, darlin', we're here. Careful not to lose your way."

I set a twenty-dollar bill under my bottle and decided not to ask for the change. Not that the food or the atmosphere was stellar, but better not to burn a bridge while I was still standing on it. I decided to save my matches for later.

"See you 'round?" Crow asked. "I'm here most days, just in case you change your mind and want some company. There's not much to do around here but drink, hunt, and play bingo."

A group of men drifted toward the billiard room. Lakota was among them and deep in conversation with a shorter man. He didn't look my way, and I took that as my cue to leave. I wasn't sure whether I would tell Hope about our chance meeting or keep it to myself until the next time Lakota swung into town. Either way, it was going on my list of weird encounters of the Shifter kind.

I smiled at Crow and grabbed the map. *"Arrivederci."*

"Music to my ears."

CHAPTER 4

"MUSIC TO MY EARS?" I muttered while driving. "What was *that* supposed to mean?" The rain had finally tapered off, but I still drove way below the speed limit so as not to miss any turns. Crow's enigmatic reply had me baffled, and I thought about what I'd said to him before leaving the bar. So I grabbed my phone and did a quick lookup of the word *arrivederci*.

"Until we meet again? Swell. All this time, I thought it meant goodbye. So much for being the educated city girl." I tossed the phone in the seat next to me. "Now he's going to think I was coming on to him."

Shifters—especially wolves—loved the dance of hard to get. Men had to prove their worth. Living with a pack had taught me that a woman should set the bar high so her suitors would work hard to win her affection.

Hopefully Crow had interpreted my fumbled remarks as disinterest and not an invitation to pursue me. The last thing I needed was some smooth-talking Shifter with a sexy smile and blue cowboy boots following me around with his tail wagging. Or worse, following me all the way back home to Austin.

I turned off the air conditioner to keep from shivering to death since my clothes were still wet. It didn't take long before the air inside the Jeep felt stuffy, especially with the humidity and heat outside. Still, a little rain was always a nice reprieve from the scorching July heat.

My stomach cramped again, reminding me to never again eat strange, improperly cooked meats. Or maybe it was the fries. Something wasn't agreeing with me, and it felt like a civil war brewing in my digestive tract.

The blinker clicked noisily as I turned right and traveled up a bumpy dirt road. Mud splashed on the undercarriage, and tiny pebbles popped against the metal frame. Signs warned against trespassing, and one cautioned to look out for venomous snakes. I had to laugh. Packs often put up signs along their property to scare away nosy humans. Then again, maybe the place really *was* infested with snakes. I shuddered at the thought. I hated snakes. Maybe *hate* was too mild a word to describe how much I loathed them.

In the dimming afternoon light, dark clouds loomed, weighted with the promise of more rain. A man walking in my direction turned a sharp eye at me. I slowed the vehicle and waved so he could get a good look and see that I wasn't a threat. His expression remained impassive, and when I continued driving, I looked in the rearview mirror and noticed a long braid down his back like the men I'd seen in the bar.

"Nice digs."

Shikoba lived in a two-story cabin of epic proportions. But to call it a cabin was a gross understatement. A long balcony stretched around the outside of the entire second floor, and it had either third-level suites or attic space. Several vehicles, though not enough to crowd the property, were parked along the tree line to the right. If they lived off the land and did most of their work out of the house, they probably had no need for more than a few. Brown gravel covered the front yard, providing traction and protecting the Jeep from the red dirt beneath.

I stared at a group of men standing on a cleared plot of land to the left. Some of them had muddy shoes and hands, and one of them twirled an axe. Had I not seen the target boards made of tree slices, I might have turned the Jeep around and called it a day.

One of the men jogged up to my Jeep and pounded his fist on the hood. I stopped the vehicle and shut off the engine. He must not have wanted me to park by their vehicles. Understandable. The last thing I wanted to do was piss these guys off by leaving a scratch on somebody's pickup.

As I hopped out, I noticed five women sitting in rocking chairs on the front porch. They were quietly talking, their eyes on me, and I had a feeling they didn't get visitors too often.

I took a step back when a ferocious-looking man with tribal markings all over the left side of his face approached me. He was a beast with a menacing presence. A man like him could easily have a lucrative career in professional wrestling.

He regarded me for a moment. "Are you Miss Church?"

I bit my lip. There must have been some kind of miscommunication.

A little girl came sprinting toward us, her pigtails bouncing like springs with every step. When she insistently tugged on the man's hand, he scooped her into his arms and anchored her against his left hip.

I shut the door. "I'm here to speak with Shikoba."

The toddler's eyes widened as she took in my hair color. I gave her a gleeful smile and bobbled my head back and forth playfully. When she reached out to touch it, the man swung away.

"Come with me," he said.

I followed him, stealing a glance at the men to my left. They stood motionless. One of them spat and turned his back to me. I had to remind myself I wasn't in Austin. If the encounter with the locals back at the bar was any indication of the fractured relationships in this community, I had a feeling they didn't trust anyone who wasn't in their tribe.

When we ascended onto the porch, the women steered their eyes away. Hope had taught me that Native Shifters were very different from the human tribes. They had their own unique languages, traditions, and way of life. Many tribes didn't welcome outsiders to live with them, especially other animals. Hope's family was an exception—an example of how the younger generations were branching off and running their packs differently. But her father still held fast to the belief that only Shifters should live in a pack, preferably wolves.

My family had different opinions on the matter.

When we entered the cabin, a double-sided stone fireplace in the center of the room drew my attention. It was flanked by simple furniture, which told me that the pack spent a lot of time socializing. The room had a lofty quality, with high ceilings and wood floors. The architecture seemed to suppress the desire to isolate oneself.

The man set the little girl down on a woven rug littered with wooden animals. She clutched a pony to her chest as I followed Mr. Beefcake to a narrow sunroom at the back of the house. It was closed off, affording privacy without the feeling of seclusion because of the tall windows that overlooked the back of the property.

An older man I presumed to be Shikoba greeted me with a nod from his brown chair. He tapped his hand on a wooden table and gestured for me to take the seat in front of him. I sat down, and the chair felt as leathery and lived-in as Shikoba's skin appeared.

After the door closed and we were alone, he plucked a blackberry from a wooden bowl and ate it. "You don't look like a Church."

"I'm Hope's partner and best friend. I came in her stead."

He pushed the bowl forward to offer me some. "I know her people. Our tribes were allies in the days of war centuries ago. Why would she not come to see me face-to-face?"

I wasn't sure what to say without inadvertently offending him, so I danced around the answer. "Our store is opening soon, and she has to finish as many designs as possible. We've fallen behind."

He licked his finger and never tore his gaze from mine.

"I'm familiar with her mother's people. Good people. What a shame her grandmother fell for such a heartless man." He tapped the rim of the bowl.

Even though my stomach was still queasy, I graciously accepted a plump blackberry. "Thank you for the honor of inviting me into your home, Mr. Shikoba."

A smirk formed on his weathered face, and his whiskey-colored eyes twinkled. Unlike the other men in the tribe, who wore single braids, Shikoba had two thin ones. A few black hairs were woven in with the grey as if they were too stubborn to concede to aging. "You can leave off the formal title. Most people call me Father or Chief, and I am neither to you."

"I'm Melody."

He chuckled and looked at my hair. "Of course you are. And tell me about your family, Melody…"

"Cole. Melody Cole. I'm recently independent, but I grew up in the Weston pack. My uncle's the Packmaster, and his brother is the beta. We're a tight family. My brothers are both alphas," I added, hoping that would impress him.

"Twin alphas," he said, connecting the dots. "Very uncommon." Shikoba hooked his finger on the bowl and dragged it toward him. "You come from a good family that sticks together. Many brothers separate because of pride."

"All of my uncles live in the same pack."

"I heard about your troubles when the war broke out. Austin Cole carries a solid reputation with the Iwa tribe. It's a shame he doesn't hold the daughters of his pack closer. Our women stay unless they choose to mate someone from another tribe."

"So they're just waiting around to get mated?" I grimaced, realizing the moment the remark flew out of my mouth that it sounded like an insult.

Shikoba plucked another blackberry from the bowl and slowly chewed on it. "Our women hunt, fish, garden, build, and help the men with teaching the children. If they choose not to mate, they will still have a place in my home. They are equals in this house. Are they not in yours?"

"We believe it causes issues if the children don't leave the home when they come of age."

His eyebrows arched knowingly. "Those issues can be easily resolved. I would much rather see the men leave my pack than the women. They are the foundation this tribe is built upon. If two men cannot resolve their differences because of their affections for the same woman, then one of them must go." His eyes flashed down to my turquoise necklace, and he admired it. "Do you know what that necklace means?"

I furrowed my brow and lifted the turtle-shaped pendant encased in silver. "Hope made it."

He picked a seed from between his teeth. "Everything we make with our hands tells a story, and if it doesn't, it's not worth having. Every small detail, every bend of the metal, every color of the stone, every imperfection—it is like reading a book. You should ask your friend someday the story that goes with that necklace you wear so frivolously around your neck. She chose a cracked stone for the body, and that is very unusual."

I hadn't realized I was touching my bracelet until his gaze skated down.

"*Sister*," he read off the metal. "Perhaps you don't need to ask after all. I wonder if your spirit animals knew each other in another life."

I nodded. *Who am I to argue?* "We heard you're one of the best and distribute top-quality stones."

"It's unfortunate for you."

"Why's that?" I asked, reaching in my purse for the notebook with our sales figures and projected earnings for the year.

"I don't deal with whiteskins."

My hopes were dashed, but I didn't have the sense he was trying to be offensive. Perhaps I just needed to win him over. Undeterred, I held a neutral expression and set the notebook on the table between us. "These are the numbers we've done so far this year. I have a monthly calculation of our profit increase as well as new-customer growth. I'm sure Hope filled you in that we're opening a store soon. We're already backed up with preorders and need to stock up our inventory."

He pushed the notebook away. "Numbers aren't important to me."

"Then what is?"

He rested his arms on the table and gave me a dispassionate look. "What do you think my people value above all else?"

Without hesitation, I answered, "Family. Loyalty."

Shikoba nodded. "Unless you have ancient tribal blood flowing in your veins, I cannot trust you. No white man has ever made a deal with my people that wasn't to benefit himself."

"I'm not those men," I said sharply, holding my ground. "I'm a wolf, and that should be trust enough. Our cultures are different, but your family's not so different from mine. We bleed for each other and fight to protect what's ours. I know the value of trust, and that's what I'm offering you."

"And what of your last supplier?" he asked, leaning back in his chair, arms folded. "Why are you in need of a replacement so close to the opening of your store?"

I mulled the question over. "He raised his prices," I said truthfully.

Shikoba dipped his chin. "And now I know how quickly you will cast me aside if I renegotiate."

I clenched my hands beneath the table, trying to quell my frustration. "We see this as a blessing in disguise. Hope doesn't want to deal with outsiders for the same reason as you. She values the relationships among the tribes and would prefer doing business with the tribes. If you raise your rates to a fair price, that's one thing. But jacking up prices because you see a golden ticket is another matter, and that's the position we were put in by our previous dealer. He was manipulating and browbeating us." I leaned forward and smoothed out the rough edges in my voice. "If I can get Hope to come up here, will you negotiate?"

He slowly shook his head.

"So this has to do with me," I said to myself, sighing deeply and lowering my head.

Even though Hope had two other guys lined up, she'd said Shikoba was her first choice. Few could secure a contract with him, and his pieces were of the finest quality—rumored to be blessed by their spiritual leaders. I'd given him my best pitch, but in the end, the real disappointment was knowing that I'd blown the deal. Hope would eventually find someone else, but she might secretly resent having partnered with me. *Am I going to be the one who held her back from the deal of a lifetime? The reason she can only sell second-rate gemstones?*

"Why didn't you just turn me away instead of inviting me in and wasting my time?"

"What kind of host would I be? How a man treats a stranger says more about his character than how he treats his family."

"What about the guy who smacks his woman around but gives a big tip to the waitress?"

Something dark flashed in his eyes. "How many packs do you know that would allow a man to beat his female? Even raise a hand to her in threat? With Shifters, masks are worn among family. You remember that, young wolf. A man will kiss his mother to keep peace within the pack, but he will always show his true face among strangers. He will berate women, disrespect his peers, and frighten children. You cannot trust a man with a painted smile and a stony heart. My mind was made up from the moment I saw you, but I respected you enough to offer my hospitality and hear what you had to say. You seem like a strong woman with a good head on your shoulders, even if your hair is the color of a wildflower that grows north of here."

The sky was darkening outside, and I glanced around for a clock.

"Is there somewhere you must be?" he asked.

I collected my notebook and tucked it back in my purse. "I need to find a motel before dusk. The roads around here are like a labyrinth, and I don't want to get lost in the dark."

Shikoba gripped a cane and rose to his feet. "You're a brave young wolf to journey so far into unfamiliar territory. That will get you far in this life. Let me show you out."

I lollygagged on my way to the door and admired the backyard. "You have a nice piece of land."

"Yes," he agreed, his feet shuffling across the floor. "It's been in my family since I was a boy."

Wow. That was certainly a long time. Shikoba must have been around eight hundred. Shifters aged slowly and lived different life spans, but most of us didn't live past a thousand. Those who lived that long were purebloods from royal lines, and not many existed since most Shifters at some point in the family tree had interbred with another animal type.

The smell of homemade bread wafted from an adjacent room as we headed to the front door. Instead of salivating, I felt a wave of nausea creep over me—probably one reason I was eager to leave the premises so hastily.

Shikoba's cane tapped on the front porch, and the women bowed to him as they went inside. A small truck was parked next to my Jeep, and when I swung my eyes to the right, a wave of terror came over me.

Lakota was standing amid the group of men, the sun catching on his bare chest. He'd stripped out of his jacket and T-shirt, leaving nothing to the imagination. His shoulders were broad and rounded with muscle, and his torso tapered down to the V in his abdomen, which I could see because of the way his jeans were slung low on his hips. His golden skin glowed, though it wasn't as dark as those who surrounded him.

Someone handed him an axe, and he hefted it for a moment before reaching over his shoulder. His bicep tightened when he threw the weapon with incredible precision. The sharp blade struck the target dead center, and cheers erupted. Lakota had always been athletically gifted—good at pool, a great swimmer, faster than most of the men in Lorenzo's pack, and not too bad at basketball either. But I'd never seen him throw a weapon before. Not like that.

Lakota's laugh was expressive, creating curved lines in his cheeks that made him all the more handsome. A cool breeze captured his long hair, and it fluttered behind his shoulders. It wasn't as straight or long as the hair of those around him, nor was it black, but those wild brown locks were always the one thing I'd loved about him. I couldn't stop noticing the predatory manner in which he moved his body, the deliberate way he turned his head to acknowledge me only to quickly look down and rejoin the conversation.

Something transpired in that split second of eye contact, and this time, I saw not just recognition in his eyes but also fear.

Shikoba looked between us and tapped his cane against my leg. "You like Sky Hunter?"

My brows knitted. "Who?"

"Lakota. The pretty one who doesn't wear a braid."

"Why do you call him Sky Hunter?"

"We gave him that nickname because he carries the sky in his eyes as a reminder of what his white ancestors want." Shikoba opened his arms wide. "Everything."

"Is he in your tribe?" I asked.

"No. He is a half blood."

"And you trust him?"

"Tribal blood will keep his wolf grounded. He runs with my pack and treats them with respect, but he's not a member of our tribe. There are rogue allies who have befriended my people, but they are not invited to live on this land unless one of my daughters takes them as a mate." After a beat, Shikoba cracked a smile. "Why don't I introduce you? He has no woman to speak of."

To speak of? I pondered that phrasing just a little too long.

"Uh, no. Thanks." I wiped my brow. "Once I find a motel, I'll give you my number there. Reception out here isn't so great on my cell. I hope you reconsider and want to talk further before I leave. Hope respects you. I don't know much about gemstones, but I trust her judgment enough to know that I want to make this work. Obviously you weren't expecting someone like me to show up at your door, but I'm a free spirit—not an irresponsible person."

Shikoba took a seat in one of the rocking chairs. "Free spirits get lost. Safe journey, Melody Cole."

Discouraged, I plodded down the stairs and across the gravel. Sweat touched my brow, and I discreetly slanted my eyes toward the men, some of whom gave me cold stares. But one man's gaze managed to set my body on fire, and for the two seconds he locked his eyes with mine, I couldn't breathe. Then I grew weak in the knees—literally.

When I hit the gravel, I heard Shikoba bellowing behind me. I couldn't make out what he said—maybe my name or something more along the lines of "Hey, interloper, get off my property! You're not a lawn ornament." I pushed myself up with one arm and snapped my head up at the men, who were stirring with quiet laughter. Lakota's expression had altered, a guarded look clouding his face. Though he turned away as if uninterested, I was certain he was watching out of the corner of his eye. If we were at home, he would have bolted toward me in a heartbeat to see if I was okay.

But we weren't at home, and he just stood there. Maybe Lakota was scouting for a pack to take him in, or maybe he wanted to mate with one of Shikoba's women. I'd been quick to assume that he was pretending not to know me because of a job, but what if the real reason had to do with the simple fact that he was embarrassed to know me? I might blow his chances if Shikoba's tribe lost respect for him because he hung out with white girls. I hadn't prepared myself for that, and it hurt.

I dragged my knee forward and prepared to stand. *Please,*

please don't let me throw up in front of everyone. My stomach twisted and spun like a carnival ride, and I instantly regretted eating the food at the bar as it finally brought on its wrath of destruction. My chest tightened, my palms became clammy, and my throat slightly expanded in such a way that signaled it was getting ready to expel unwanted contents. *Focus, Mel. Focus. Not in front of Shikoba. Not now.*

Footsteps approached from behind me, accompanied by the distinct sound of a wooden cane tapping against the gravel. "Sky Hunter, come help this woman."

"I'm dirty," Lakota said gruffly.

"Do as I say," Shikoba commanded, inviting no argument.

Lakota exchanged glances with the men standing by him then swiped his T-shirt off the ground. As he sauntered toward us, I could sense his reluctance to help.

I swung my gaze down, my legs shaky as I stood up. "I don't need any help. Something just made me dizzy for a minute."

Lakota feigned a smirk. "Maybe we should put our shirts back on."

I glared at him as I scooped my purse and dignity off the ground. "Don't flatter yourself."

Shikoba studied my face and shook his head as he came to some conclusion. "Drive this woman and show her the way to the motel."

"How do you propose I get back?"

"Take a room there," he replied, stepping close and lowering his voice. "It's a bad omen if she dies after visiting my land and eating our food. Her sickness or death will bring trouble. You must take her off this land, or else her spirit will latch on to us in the afterlife."

"Whoa," I said, raising my hands. "Let's not plan my funeral just yet. Something I ate at the bar didn't agree with me. I just need to lie down for a little while, and I'll be as right as rain."

Ignoring me, Shikoba continued giving Lakota orders. "I'll send Tak over in the morning with your truck."

"Someone's growing roots over there," one of the men razzed. "The bet's not over, Sky Hunter. You still have one more throw."

Lakota yelled back, sounding like someone who'd just received punishment. "I'll see you boys later. I have to babysit."

"Careful not to turn your back on that one," another called. "She's a trickster."

"Nice friends you got there," I murmured as we headed to the Jeep.

When we reached the driver's-side door, he got in, and I stood there for a moment, staring at him through the window. Still too queasy to give him the finger, I shuffled around to the other side, irritated by his lack of manners. It wasn't that Lakota was the shining example of a gentleman, but he'd always respected women. That was what his parents had taught him as a child.

But apparently he'd grown up to become a jackass.

Wondering why the fates were punishing me, I climbed in and buckled my seat belt. Without a word, Lakota backed out and turned around. We passed a few more of Shikoba's packmates along the dirt road, and they watched with curiosity.

Ignoring the awkward silence, I searched the glove compartment before reaching beneath my seat. There had to be a plastic sack *somewhere* that I could use to get sick in. My stomach took precedence over everything else, including having a conversation with someone I hadn't seen in years.

"What are you looking for?" he asked curtly.

I closed my eyes, struggling to think about something that would take my mind off this terrible feeling. But the more I tried to pretend it wasn't happening, the more my mouth began to water and my stomach began to churn. Every bump in the road became torture.

"Pull over," I croaked.

"You look green."

When I unhooked my seat belt and gripped the door handle, the truck lurched to the right and came to a hard stop. Without a second to spare, I flung open the door and stumbled into the high grass. It was as if the smell of fresh air had given my body permission to release, and I bent over, every muscle contracting as my stomach offered a full return on lunch.

My vision blurred with tears, but the humiliation hadn't quite sunk in yet. It was just a physical reaction, and I had no doubt that my eyeliner was officially everywhere. I walked farther out and dropped to my knees.

I swear to the fates I'll only eat prepackaged food on my next road trip, I vowed, heaving once more. *Donuts, pizza, potato chips.*

Wiping my face, I cleared my mind. "Stop thinking about food."

Before I knew what was happening, Lakota was behind me, holding my hair back with one hand. But by then I was done and just needed a minute to collect myself. He must have sensed that and let go. My hair curtained my face, allowing no breeze to offer me any relief.

When I finally stood up and turned around, my jaw slackened. Lakota had ditched me and was getting into the Jeep.

It wasn't until he tapped the horn that I knew I wanted to slap him.

CHAPTER 5

A S SOON AS WE ARRIVED at a cheap motel, I went to the main office, checked in, and headed straight to my room. After the scenic stop on mile marker fifty, I felt remarkably better but still not back to my old self. What I needed was to sleep and recharge. I would have liked to shift, but since that wasn't an option, I filled the sink with hot water, submerged my tank top and socks, then crawled into bed and wrapped myself in a cocoon.

Though I was tired, my mind wouldn't stop racing. If only Shikoba had given us a chance—a trial period to prove we could work together. I didn't have the courage to tell Hope that the real reason she wasn't getting the best gemstone dealer in North America was because of me. I hadn't just failed to secure a deal—I'd failed my best friend.

When my phone rang, I groaned beneath the covers. It had to be Hope. I could just let it ring, but then she would worry. *What am I going to say?* Our store was opening in a week, and if she didn't have any luck with the other two guys, we were screwed.

I squirmed out of my cocoon and answered. "Hello?"

"Mel, I've been trying to reach you," Hope said, her voice shaky. "Are you all right?"

I kicked the covers away. "I got food poisoning from the worst roadside burger in history. How was your day?"

"I had lunch with the dealer. We never made it back to his place."

I snorted. "Didn't get lucky?"

"Don't be silly. We sat inside a Mexican restaurant at the River Walk. It's so hot down here. The fans were blowing, but it didn't help."

After putting the phone on speaker, I rested it on my stomach. "You should have come up here instead. You would have gotten to enjoy a nice electrical storm and a rain shower."

"Maybe the fates are trying to tell us something," she said absently. "I cut the meeting short because I didn't get a good vibe from the man. Maybe he has a good reputation with some people, but he's hiding something. There's a mark on his character I couldn't put my finger on. Some of his answers were evasive, and others were chosen with fastidious care."

I stayed quiet, praying she'd continue.

"Mel? Do you have good news to share?"

The hopefulness in her voice about killed me, and I shielded my eyes. "I'm staying overnight, and I plan to talk to him again in the morning."

"Again? Oh, Mel. What happened?"

When the door suddenly opened, my entire body jolted as if hit with an electric shock. The phone flipped onto the bed, and I immediately pressed my hands over my black bra.

"Melody?" Hope called out. "Did I lose you?"

Lakota pressed his index finger against his lips and quietly closed the door. When he turned to secure the drapes, I grabbed the phone.

"I'm here. Don't worry if you can't reach me. The connection up here sucks. I'll call you when I have news."

"All right then. As long as you're okay. I'll be heading up to Waco tomorrow and will give you an update then."

Just as soon as the words left her mouth, Lakota jerked his chin at me, fire dancing in his eyes. *Alone?* he mouthed.

"Talk soon." I quickly ended the call and set the phone

on the nightstand. "It's a business trip. Unlike me, she's in the company of civilized people."

He stalked toward the bed and crawled onto it, planting a fist on either side of me and pinning me with his gaze. His brown hair fell forward, framing his face, and the ends were damp and clumped together.

"You smell like rain," I said, forgetting to put the filter between my innermost thoughts and my mouth.

Lakota's hair had grown since I'd last seen him. He was bent down low enough that it tickled my face as I stared into his narrowing eyes.

"What are you doing here?" he growled slowly.

I'd never been more aware that I was half-naked beneath a man until that moment. "I had a business meeting with Shikoba. The real question is: what are *you* doing here, *Sky Hunter*?"

His eyes twinkled, and for a moment, I saw the old Lakota flickering in their depths. "Why is my sister traveling alone to Waco? And don't skip over the part where she said *up* to Waco. Up from where?"

I tried shoving at his chest to throw him off, but it was like pushing a boulder. Instead, I wriggled down and crawled out from beneath him. I snatched a pillow and hugged it against my body, my feet wide apart and my chin held high. "Because your sister has one week to secure a new gemstone dealer before all hell breaks loose. We're up to our ears in preorders and don't have enough inventory to last through the next quarter. Especially with the time it takes for her to make those pieces. The guy she was using flaked out on us, and now we're in a crunch." I looked down and smoothed out the wrinkles in the pillow I was clutching. "She drove down to San Antonio, and that didn't work out. We've got one more prospect in Waco, but I'm not holding my breath."

Lakota was still on all fours, and it was a titillating image. Unable to wait for his answer, I stumbled backward into the bathroom and slammed the door.

What is wrong with you? I scolded my reflection in the mirror. Even as I stood there trying to collect my thoughts, I imagined him still on the bed, waiting for my return. And that thought sent tingles between my legs. Renegade desire pulsed through me. I sure as heck wasn't in heat, not unless all the stress was somehow inducing it.

The faucet squeaked when I turned it on. As I splashed cold water onto my face, I replayed the scene from the moment he walked into the room. Something about his scent was intoxicating, and it wasn't the rainwater. The nearer he came to me, the more I felt power in his presence. It must have been his wolf I was sensing. Or pheromones. Lakota was no alpha, but he was a born leader who, if he chose to, could help lead a pack as a second-in-command. My uncle Reno had the same effect on people. So did William, just not to the same degree. Maybe it was his amicable personality.

Lakota's energy was raw and unbending, making my wolf immediately want to submit to his command. And I didn't like submitting to anyone. *What would have happened had I not wriggled free from beneath him? Would he still have me pinned, trying to dominate my wolf? Would he have settled his body on top of mine? What would it feel like to have Lakota's weight come down on me, his teeth nipping at my neck?*

"Best friend's brother, best friend's brother," I kept whispering to myself.

I stared at my tank top floating in the sink. Since this trip was only supposed to have been for a day, it hadn't occurred to me when leaving that I might need a change of clothes. I snatched a white towel from the rack and tied it around my torso, ready to face Lakota and finally get some answers about what he was doing in a small town called Running Horse.

But when I swung the bathroom door open, Lakota was gone.

The news lady on the television spoke about another unidentified body found by the tracks, gas prices, then segued to a video of a local woman who had just turned one hundred. I finished towel-drying my wet hair before using the towel to wipe some of the fog off the mirror in front of me.

After Lakota had vanished from my motel room, I'd taken a shower and hung my tank top on the towel rack to dry. Even though I hadn't planned an overnight trip, I'd put an extra pair of panties in my purse just in case. I could have brought emergency clothes, but I didn't want to lug around a bag, and wearing the same outfit for two days in a row wasn't anything new in my life.

Oh, what to do about this Shikoba situation? I'd outright lied to Hope when I told her I planned to see him in the morning. But if I actually *did* go, would it still be a lie? Maybe that wasn't such a terrible idea. It would give me time to think of a better approach.

I looked at my reflection. All the smeared eyeliner and lipstick was gone, so without makeup, my freckles were noticeable. I was born with pouty lips, but they were more swollen than usual after I'd nibbled on them so much in the past hour.

My fingers traced over my black bra, the fabric too big since my breasts didn't fill the cups completely. *Did Lakota notice the woman I've become?* My waist was no longer as narrow as a pencil, and aside from my colorful hair, there was nothing childlike in my features. I was a full-fledged Shifter. *Could he sense the wolf inside me?*

As I hooked my thumbs in my black bikini bottom, I remembered the lustful looks when I'd entered the bar earlier. Then I thought about the way Shikoba's tribe had looked at me indifferently. And Lakota was one of them. I didn't fit their mold of beauty. Hell, I didn't seem to fit anyone's.

I sighed and flipped off the light before padding into the bedroom. Normally I didn't sleep in a bra, but my plan was to sit up for a while. Though my stomach was all right, my head was throbbing from dehydration. I'd somehow managed to build up an appetite again, but the area didn't have any places to eat that I'd noticed. I turned in a circle, searching for my pants. I'd *made* those pants, and the last place I wanted them was lying on the dirty floor of a motel room.

Just as I bent over to collect them, hinges squeaked behind me. With my ass to the door, I frantically lifted my pants to cover my chest and whirled around.

Lakota stood frozen, eyes wide, a sack in one hand and the card key in the other. "Uh…" He quickly turned around and shut the door, still facing the wall. "I thought you were, uh—"

"Don't you knock?" I quickly stepped into my jeans and yanked them up. With my tank top still drying in the bathroom, I clutched the pillow and hugged it tight. "I thought you left."

"I had to move the Jeep and grab a few things."

"Why do you have my key?"

"Can I turn around?"

I rested my chin on the top of the pillow. "Yes."

He set the bag on the table and held up the card. "I didn't want you sneaking out while I was gone." He flicked it next to his phone and strode toward me.

Each step he took made my heart fall to the same rhythm. "Wh-What are you doing?" I sputtered. "I'm not dressed."

As he rounded the bed, he slowly peeled off his white T-shirt with a black arrowhead printed on the front and held it between his fingers. "Put this on."

When Lakota turned around, I slipped into his tight shirt, which hung loose on my body. It smelled like him, and I resisted pulling the fabric up to my nose and drawing in a deep breath. Staring at his muscular back wasn't helping my self-control either.

"How did you get in the first time?" I asked.

"It's an old motel. When you close the door, you need to lift the handle all the way back into place, or it doesn't shut.

That's why a lot of shady stuff goes down in this place and why Shikoba sent me here to protect you."

I flipped my hair out from beneath the collar.

"Ready?" he asked.

When he turned, I casually tucked my hands in my pockets.

He cocked his head to the side and studied me closely. "Little Melody's all grown-up."

"I've *been* grown-up."

"Tall, yes. Grown-up? No. When did you go through your first change?"

"What makes you think I have?"

He leaned in slowly and drew in a deep breath. When he spoke, his voice was smoky and quiet. "Because my wolf can smell it."

I shivered and stepped back. "Is that why you were sniffing me back at the bar?"

Lakota chuckled and arched an eyebrow. "You haven't changed."

Jerking my head toward the table, I asked, "What's in the bag?"

"That depends." Lakota reached out unexpectedly and tucked my hair behind my ears. It wasn't a gesture meant to be affectionate; he was trying to get a better look at my eyes. "How are you feeling?"

I pulled my hands from my pockets and shrugged. "Better, I guess."

He ensnared my wrist and led me toward the table by the door. "Good. I want you to eat something before you go to bed. You have a long drive home in the morning."

I twisted my arm out of his grasp. "I'm not leaving in the morning."

"Yes, you are," he said, his response annoyingly succinct. When he unrolled the top of the sack, he pulled out a loaf of bread, smooth peanut butter, grape jelly, and a bag of chips.

My eyes widened as I watched in stunned silence. Lakota

hadn't left my motel room because he didn't want me to be his problem anymore—he'd just gone to bring me food, and the fact that he was providing for me made my wolf stir just a little bit.

"Sour cream and onion," I said, nodding at the chips. "That should make my breath smell nice."

He gave me a sideways glance. "Are you planning on kissing someone?" Lakota sighed and looked down at his offering. "Your wolf is probably craving meat."

I splayed my fingers across my stomach and sat on the edge of the bed. "She's going to have to wait. Thanks to the local cuisine, my stomach has trust issues at the moment." While he twisted open the bag of bread and began making a sandwich, I decided to address the elephant in the room. "Are you working undercover?"

"Yes."

Relief washed over me. He still wasn't being his usual self, but at least I had a definitive answer for why he'd ignored me. Deciding not to reveal that Hope had confided his secret to me, I said, "I haven't seen you in a long time, so I kind of figured as much. Is there a reason I shouldn't trust Shikoba? I'm down here trying to close a deal with him, but if he's under investigation for a crime, then maybe that's something I should know."

He gave me a cross look while pouring the potato chips onto my paper plate. "You don't belong here."

"So I gathered from the friendly welcome wagon. If you can't tell me why you're here, can you at least tell me if Shikoba is a man your sister can trust doing business with?"

He pulled out a chair. "Sit down, and we'll talk."

The lamp by the bed was on the low setting, and it somehow made our conversation more intimate. When I drifted over to take a seat, he pushed my chair in like a gentleman—a far cry from the man who, in front of all his buddies, had hopped into my Jeep without opening my door.

Lakota sat across from me and put the sack on the floor.

He reached into the potato chip bag, grabbed a handful of chips, and dropped them onto a paper plate in front of him. "You can trust Shikoba. He's a good man with integrity and honor. I respect him."

I pushed his phone aside. "He turned me away because I'm not native. Their behavior isn't normal. I've never experienced this kind of animosity between people just because of their skin color or heritage. Usually it's packs not trusting cougars or something along those lines."

"The tribe doesn't hate nontribes. They just don't understand them. They've been wronged in the past, and since they've lived here all their lives, what else can they do but draw from their own experience? That's how it is in small towns, and it's hard to weed out the prejudices when your life span is centuries. People hang on to the past. Shikoba barely trusts me, and it took a long time to earn his acceptance. He would never have let me in if I didn't have the same blood running in my veins. My blue eyes remind him to stay guarded."

"You should have worn contacts."

Lakota pursed his lips for a moment and rubbed his neck. "I thought about it, but if one of them fell out, it would look like I'm hiding something. If any good comes from this, maybe he'll learn that he can trust someone who isn't like him. Small changes start with ripples."

"You're starting to sound like your mother." When I bit into my sandwich, I heaved a sigh and relaxed.

"Nobody eats the food at that bar," Lakota said with a chuckle. "I knew you were in trouble when I saw you scarfing down those fries."

"*Now* you warn me."

He reached into the sack and produced a can of root beer. I tamped down the urge to smile because I was still a little mad at him. Lakota hadn't just selected random food out of the store—he'd specifically chosen foods that I liked. Root beer had always been a favorite of mine.

He crossed his arms on the table and gave me a pointed

stare. "Now that you're old enough to be traveling on your own, I should warn you about Breed bars. What goes down in Austin isn't the same as the rest of the world, especially not in the backwoods. You don't have a pack to protect you, and an unfamiliar face only titillates Shifters who've been staring at the same people day in and day out. Don't invite anyone into your space. Wolves can scent a fresh bitch. Not everyone out here plays by the rules, and you need to know that. I'm surprised Lennon and Hendrix let you come."

"They miss you," I said. "They were asking about their fishing buddy just the other day."

Lakota laughed heartily and showed off his megawatt smile. "We're too old for fishing in the river. If you put all three of us in a canoe, we would sink to the bottom."

I laughed at the mental image. My brothers had grown into strong men, and it seemed like just yesterday they were playing games and climbing trees.

Lakota's laughter faded, and he stared at his chips. "Have they thought about starting a pack?"

I cracked open the can of root beer and washed down the sandwich. After a small burp, I wiped my mouth and set the can between us. "It's too soon for them to become Packmasters. Plus... it's hard for them. It means they'll have to split up, and they've never been apart."

"They'll make a strong alliance if they choose the right men for their packs." Lakota crunched loudly on a potato chip and then licked his finger. "Have you thought about joining with one of them?"

I lowered my eyes. Lennon and Hendrix meant the world to me, and while neither of them had brought up the topic, it was one I felt strongly about. "I would have to choose," I said. "How can I choose between two brothers I love equally and not expect one of them to take it personally?"

"Your old pack is growing," he pointed out. "More children will come. Do you think they won't want to join? Packs are stronger when family members are a part of them. The trust is already there. It's not a matter of choosing sides. Family forges a stronger loyalty."

"I know, but still. It's not the same with their cousins. I'm their sister, and it feels like I'm choosing who's the better brother."

"Admit it," he pressed. "You'd join one of their packs in a heartbeat if they asked. There's a sense of security you'll have with your brother being the Packmaster. He'll look out for you and protect you like no one else will."

"True. But the perks wouldn't be worth hurting someone who loves me. They have another destiny to follow, and I have a feeling I'm not going to be a part of it. I wouldn't hesitate if I just had one alpha brother, but instead I have two. Something I've learned over the years is how alpha twins are especially sensitive to favoritism. My family tries to stop them from small competitions. No matter how much they love each other, they have an innate desire to stand apart. People might try to make me feel guilty over not choosing, but no one has walked in my shoes."

"True," he agreed, steepling his fingers in front of his face. His gaze drifted to the side. "But choosing neither is also making a statement."

A question sat on the tip of my tongue. I pondered whether I should ask it or let the silence build between us. Lakota was speaking from a position of inexperience, having not grown up in a pack. I wouldn't be able to understand his remarks without learning how his upbringing had shaped his point of view. His adoptive parents weren't even Shifters, let alone the same Breed, and even though he'd often traveled down to visit with his birth mother, he didn't have a clue what it was like to live in a pack. Yet he so freely gave advice on it.

I mustered a little courage to speak honestly with him. "What was it like not growing up in a pack?"

Lakota fooled around with a small radio sitting on the table. He rolled the dial until the static cleared. "Time After Time" came on and dissolved the tension between us.

"I had a fortunate life," he began. "Two fathers, two mothers, and more family than I could hope for. If my chosen parents hadn't saved me from the black market, who knows where I'd be now. A slave—of that I have no doubt. They couldn't legally adopt, and yeah, some frown upon what they did, but black marketeers sell to high-paying criminals, and nothing can stop them. There are men out there who want kids they can groom as killers or brainwashed lackeys. I can't judge my parents for the love they gave me, even if it came at a price. I grew up in a stable home with different Breeds. I grew up with love and acceptance." Lakota folded his arms on the table. "No, I wasn't born and bred in a pack, but I have a better perspective on the world than most people."

I stared at my empty plate. I'd never asked Lakota why his birth mother had given him away. Since even Hope hadn't brought it up with me, I knew it was none of my business. In fact, I never really questioned why Hope had a brother who lived in another state. It was so normal that it wasn't until I was older that I began to look at their family structure and realize there was more to the story. My pack seemed to know the history, but it wasn't a detail they ever shared with me.

"Your mother put you on the black market?"

His lip curled. "She would have never done that. It wasn't her choice."

Sensing his agitation, I decided his past was too heavy a subject to discuss over a sandwich. "I bet your parents miss you."

Lakota smiled, tilting his head to the side. "Which ones?"

"All."

He leaned back in his chair, arms hooked over the back corners. "And what about yours? I thought your father would have hired bodyguards by now for his little girl."

I snorted. "Don't put the idea in his head. Did Hope ever tell you that the first week we moved out, he was sleeping in the alley across the street from our apartment? He lied to my mother and said he was out of town, recording an album with his band. True story."

Lakota threw back his head and laughed, and it was warm and full-bodied. "How did you find out?"

"One night I ran out to pick up Mexican food and took a shortcut. Tripped right over him." I started laughing on the last word, and Lakota joined in.

It felt good to fall back into our old relationship.

Familiar.

Easy.

He leaned forward and threaded his fingers through his hair. "Mind if I call my sis?"

"Just don't tell her you're with me. That'll raise all kinds of questions."

When Lakota reached for his phone, his finger brushed against mine. After a few swipes on the screen, he held the phone to his ear and turned away. "How's my baby sister?" Then he laughed. "I miss you too. Everything's fine. Where are you?"

I touched the spot where his finger had grazed, curious about my reaction. I subtly searched his body for tattoos or scars, but unless his hair was covering one or he liked tramp stamps, his torso wasn't marked with ink. Perhaps that was a smart move for a bounty hunter since a tattoo would make him easy to identify.

"Of course I am," he said, his voice sweeter than before. "Now tell me why you're in Waco."

When his eyes slanted toward mine, I quickly studied a crack in the ceiling.

"You haven't told Father?" he chided.

Poor Hope. I had my hands full with twin brothers, but they were younger than I was. Only in recent years had they finally grown into men, so I couldn't imagine having grown up with an older brother who constantly stuck his nose in my business. Lakota had always been her protector, even from miles away. It made me wonder if Shikoba had it all wrong about how a man treats a stranger. Lakota had always looked out for Hope, and he wasn't doing it to impress anyone. No one had ever expected him to be so involved in her life since he lived across the country and didn't share the same father with her, but he was. I couldn't even recall a single instance when she needed him and he wasn't there. Not when he was ten and especially not now that he was thirty.

While they caught up, I bent over and peered into the paper bag to see if there was another drink.

"What the heck?" I hooked my finger on the edge and dragged the sack toward me. Magazines, a toothbrush, toothpaste, antacids, a giant bottle of water...

Lakota reached out and snatched the bag away, the phone still to his ear. "If you have an emergency, call me. Go straight home after the meeting. If it's close to dark, then I want you to find a nice hotel. ... Don't worry—I'll reimburse you. Do you know anything about this male you're meeting up with?" Lakota gave me another scolding glance while Hope must have been talking his ear off to pacify him. "Uh-huh. And if she doesn't?"

I hooked my arms on the back of the chair and coolly tilted my head to the side. *Does he really think this was all my doing?*

He fished his hand in his pocket and pulled out a black band. "You do that. And carry the pepper spray I gave you. Okay, love you too." He set the phone on the bedside table and raised his arms to tie his hair in a bun.

I'd never found man buns attractive until the moment he turned to look at me. His face was no longer obscured by all that hair, and I could really take in how much he had changed. High cheekbones drew all the attention to his lustrous blue eyes, and his complexion was warmer than usual, amplified by the summer sun. Lakota had a pensive brow and a broad mouth with soft lips. At least, they looked soft. I could definitely see where his Native American features warred with something else.

He stood up and reached in the sack, eyes still on mine. When he pulled his arm free, he was holding a bottle of mustard.

I grinned. "You remembered."

"How could I forget? You're the only person I've ever known who eats it straight out of the bottle." Lakota set it in front of me and stood so close that I could feel his wolf's power vibrating against my skin.

He wanted my approval.

When I reached for the bottle, our hands touched briefly. Before I could register that my stomach was getting that fluttery feeling, I twisted the top off, peeled back the lid, screwed the cap back on, shook the bottle, and squirted the mustard straight into my mouth.

Lakota shook his head with a tight grin. "Disgusting."

After swallowing, I set the bottle on the table. "If you think that's gross, you should see my Shifter craving." Suddenly embarrassed, I licked the corner of my mouth and looked down, only to find myself staring at his abs. Deciding that was even more awkward, I dragged my gaze back up to his eyes. "Thanks for bringing me all this stuff. I'll pay you back."

He reached out and swiped mustard from my lips. "No worries. Get some rest. I'll swing by in the morning and see you off."

But I had no plans to leave right away, and I wasn't certain whether it had more to do with Shikoba or the wolf standing before me.

"Good night, Sky Hunter."

Lakota walked past me and opened the door. "Good night, Freckles," he murmured quietly.

CHAPTER 6

M Y WOLF WAS BOUNDING THROUGH the dark woods, her paws sinking into wet earth and leaving behind muddy footprints. Her throat was parched, legs aching, heart beating at a wicked pace. It wasn't the scent of pine or soil in her nose—it was fear. When she turned to look over her shoulder, I glimpsed a dark shadow gaining on us. The clouds blackened as a vortex spun in a slow circle, the ominous storm threatening to destroy everything.

Gasping, I shot up in bed. My heart raced out of control as I glanced around at unfamiliar surroundings. It wasn't my bed or my home, and I didn't recognize the smell. Dim light filtered through a gap in the heavy drapes on my right. I glanced down at my hands, expecting to see paws caked in mud. But I wasn't in the forest or in wolf form. It took a minute or two for the dream to shake off, but remembering I was in a human motel didn't calm me in the least. If I shifted, someone might take it upon themselves to shoot me and use my pelt for decorating their cabin floor. I shuddered at the thought.

Loud chattering outside my window caught my attention. Unable to hear the conversation, I swung my legs over the edge of the bed and approached the window. Through the slim opening in the drapes, I saw three men hanging out on the walkway in front of my room, laughing and talking about a truck show. My wolf must have heard them and sensed danger. Thank the fates I hadn't shifted.

When a fist pounded against my door, I froze in terror. I stared down at my bare legs and panicked.

"Open up, honey," Lakota said.

Honey? I blew out a breath. When I unlocked the door, he pushed his way inside and closed it. Then he peered through the curtains, still shirtless. At least he had his pants on.

"What are you doing in here?" I hissed.

He kept his voice low. "I don't like the way those men have been hanging around in front of your door for the past hour."

I rubbed my eyes and yawned. "How would you know?"

"Keep your voice down," he said. "I don't know if they saw you or not, but if they think a white girl is in here with me, there'll be trouble if they hear us arguing."

Groaning, I crawled back into bed. "What century is this? I've been to Oklahoma several times, and I've never seen such a blatant display of racism."

"You're on the edge of Shifter territory," he said, moving away from the window. "Where worlds collide."

"How can you stand it?"

He sniffed. "Don't be so quick to lump me in with these people. I blend because I have to, not because I want to."

I rolled to the other side of the bed. "You can lie down next to me if you like. I mean… until the serial killers outside my room leave."

All I could see were his silhouette and his hesitation. "Maybe you should put your pants on."

"I can't sleep in jeans."

"I should go."

"Then go."

A curtain of silence fell between us.

"I can't go," he said, his voice rough. "Those men are still there."

Tickled, I pulled the sheet to my chin. "Do you want me to get my bow out of the car and protect you?"

Though I couldn't see his smile, I knew it was there.

The bed dipped low when he anchored his knee on it and flopped onto his back. His shoes hit the floor one at a time. As my eyes began to adjust to what little light was in the room, his profile came into view. Lakota's expression was inscrutable, his eyes fixed on the ceiling as he laced his fingers across his chest.

"What are you thinking about?" I asked.

"Do you really wanna know?"

"I wouldn't ask if I didn't."

He hesitated for a moment. "That night in the snowstorm... when I found you. I think about it a lot."

I also spent many nights thinking about it but probably for different reasons. "Why?"

"I don't know," he said. "It changed me somehow. When I found you, my wolf felt at peace. I haven't known that kind of peace since. No matter how many cases I break or how many people I rescue, he's always restless."

"Maybe he's a dancer trapped in a bounty hunter's body."

Lakota chortled and wiped his forehead. "Why's it so damn hot in here?"

"The AC is broken."

He turned his head toward me slowly, deliberately. "Why didn't you tell me that earlier?"

"I wasn't hot earlier. It's not worth complaining about if I have to get up in a few hours. What time is it?"

"One."

"Aren't you afraid of blowing your cover by staying in my room?"

Lakota averted his eyes, a conflicted look on his face. "If the tribe finds out, I'll tell them you were sick and I had to stay to make sure you didn't keel over from Red's cooking."

I quirked an eyebrow and brought my arm out from beneath the covers. "Oh? Is *that* what you'll tell Shikoba's men? Or will your version be that you and I had hot sex in a motel room? That would be a juicy story for your friends, not to mention taboo in their eyes."

He turned on his side to face me, his hair no longer bound but free and draped across his neck. "Don't mention any of this when you go back home. Hope knows better than to ask questions, but I can't afford anyone knowing I'm here. Word spreads like wildfire, and it wouldn't take long before I was exposed."

The humor faded, eclipsed by the gravity of the situation. I rolled over, our faces close enough that I could feel his breath. "I might joke around, but I would never do anything to put your life in danger."

The chatter died down outside, and the footsteps of the men faded.

Lakota peered over his shoulder at the window. "I should go. My wolf needs to run."

"Then take your shirt," I said. "You can't be running around shirtless in the morning."

A smile was in his voice when he said, "Can't I?"

Before he could argue, I stripped out of the white tee and handed it over. The energy between us shifted in such a palpable way that heat licked down my body. His eyes latched onto my bra before traveling down to my navel, where the sheet was tucked around my waist. Nudity among Shifters was a part of life, and what I had on was the equivalent of a bikini, which Lakota had seen many times when we went swimming at the lake. But we were kids then, and lying beneath the covers just inches away from him reminded me of how much we had changed. The way he looked at me was unfamiliar and provocative. I wasn't sure whether it was him looking at me that way or his wolf.

"Do you normally wear your bra to sleep?"

I smiled. "I sometimes forget I have it on."

"Have you ever been with a man?"

"That's a little personal." I pulled the sheet up to my chin.

"Maybe I just want to know if your brothers are looking out for you."

I rose up on my elbow. "My brothers look out for me just fine. But that doesn't include dictating who I sleep with."

"Maybe it should." His tone was cocksure and threaded with judgment. "You shouldn't go around sleeping with men unless it matters. Especially before joining a pack. That kind of reputation is damning in a Packmaster's eyes, whether you're male or female."

"First of all, I don't just go around sleeping with random men. Secondly, it mattered. At least I thought it did at the time."

"What happened?"

I relaxed my arm and tucked it beneath my head. "I guess I didn't matter to them. Or maybe we didn't matter together."

"Is that all?"

Smiling, I said, "That's my story, and I'm stickin' to it."

The truth was more shameful to admit. None of my sexual encounters had been electric or emotionally intense. I'd cared for those men, and while the sex had felt good, something was always lacking in the relationship. Their touch hadn't set me on fire. A suggestive glance hadn't made me hunger for their affection. I was a sexual creature, but I'd spent more time fantasizing about hot sex than actually having it.

Maybe I would never find a man who set my body ablaze with a heated look—someone who would also care about what was in my head and not just in my pants. None of those guys cared about my clothing design. *Am I asking for too much?*

"What about you, Romeo? What's the real reason you're working undercover jobs? I bet you're hiding from the trail of tears you've left behind. How many hearts have you broken?"

"You don't think much of me," he said decidedly. "I respect women more than that."

"Come on," I groaned. "No one leaves a relationship happy. It's always a bitter breakup. Unless you're one of those guys who doesn't do relationships. Just has sex recreationally.

Although, if that's true, you're not exactly in a position to judge women who sleep around. Not saying I'm one of those women, but..."

He rose hastily on his elbow. "I'm a virgin."

Before my synapses had an opportunity to process that information, Lakota rolled over and showed me his back.

Dumbstruck, I thought, *Is he kidding? Is this one of his jokes?* Men like Lakota weren't virgins. Everyone knew he'd gone through his first change in his teens, much earlier than boys usually did. Every time he came to town, the girls were preening and throwing themselves at him with coy smiles and salacious glances. He'd gone out on dates with several beautiful girls with less than stellar reputations. No, Lakota wasn't a virgin. That would be like saying the earth was flat.

I sat up. "Don't say things like that just to make me feel like a slut. I've slept with men, but that doesn't mean I sleep around. It's a double standard to expect women to live by some moral code that doesn't apply to you."

"I need to go." He swung his feet to the floor and stood up.

Before he could make it to the door, I scrambled out of bed and went after him. "Wait a minute. Are you playing some kind of a game with me? Why are you being so aloof?"

He spun around, his ferocity staggering. "Aloof?"

I suddenly forgot that I was standing in nothing but panties and a bra. "Yeah, *aloof.* I can understand pretending not to know me in front of your buddies—you're undercover. But when I was sick on the side of the road, you took off and actually blew the horn at me to hurry up. That's not the Lakota I remember." I circled around him and blocked the door. "You've changed."

He reduced the space between us and dipped his chin. "I couldn't risk someone seeing. The woods have eyes."

I sputtered with laughter. "And what could they have possibly witnessed that would have blown your cover?"

When he touched his forehead to mine, I froze. "My affection for you," he said on a breath.

My shoulders sagged. "Still the same old jokester you always were. Except now your jokes aren't so funny."

As I walked around him, he captured my wrist and yanked me against him. Without warning, Lakota's mouth was on mine, his kiss hot. His arms encircled my waist, then branched apart until one rested on the base of my spine and the other cradled my nape. I tried to resist, but I was caught in a storm I couldn't escape. His lips were sensual—pliant yet firm as they asked and they gave all at once. I absorbed every inch of his body against mine, discarding all rational thought.

My legs parted as I yearned to know him intimately. Lakota's velvety tongue stroked against mine, teaching me how provocative a kiss could be. He branded me with his mouth—fingers curling against my skin, breath heavy, energy pulsing like a heartbeat. I splayed my hands across his strong shoulders to steady myself—to give me something to hold on to so I didn't float away. Each swipe of his tongue grew more eager than the last, and he seduced me with his taste, his heady scent, his fervid touch.

Then a word entered my mind.

Virgin.

His hands and mouth showed no indication of inexperience. Was I supposed to believe his admission that he'd never claimed a woman?

As our kiss deepened, I became attuned to the subtle changes in his body—the way his breath hitched each time I swiped my thumb across his nipple, how his heart galloped when I nibbled on his bottom lip. It left me uncertain about what the truth really was. So much hunger was in his touch—yet so much restraint. He kept his hands locked in place, holding me against him. They didn't eagerly go for my bra strap or slide inside my panties.

"Lakota," I whispered, though it sounded more like a whimper.

He drew back, his breath heavy. "Am I hurting you?"

Hurting? His lips were like a pledge against mine. "Were you serious about what you said?"

He inclined his head, the passion crumbling from his expression. "I can't talk about this with you."

I took his wrist. "You're the one who started it. If it's true, I won't tell anyone. But I also don't want you saying hurtful things to make a point about my past relationships. I'm not a stranger. I'm not some girl you just met. It's me... Melody. I've known you my entire life. *Talk* to me."

In the dark shadows of the motel room, Lakota gave me his confession. His hesitation and embarrassment confirmed that he had never spoken those words before to anyone, and it made me wonder why he'd brought it up. Maybe he'd kept it bottled up for so long that he needed to get it off his chest. "It's true. I've never been with a woman."

I stripped away all judgment from the tone of my voice. "By choice?"

"My fathers have different views on courting a woman. My adoptive father is a Chitah, so he tells me that courtship matters above all else. But..." Lakota walked around to sit on the edge of the bed.

I sat to his right, my hand on his leg. "You can tell me anything. I promise it won't leave this room. It's just between us."

"My stepfather believes bedding a woman makes a Shifter a man. That's what most Shifters believe. I haven't told him, but he knows. Somehow... he knows and thinks lesser of me because of it."

I could understand his being a virgin at twenty. But *thirty?* Lakota was a virile wolf, and it made no sense.

"How far have you gone?"

He shrugged lightly. "Kissing. Some light petting. Nothing sexual."

I blinked in surprise. "That's it? But all those girls you dated..."

Lakota sighed. "I was young then, and it didn't take long for me to figure out how good touch felt. But I was afraid I'd lose control, so I quit dating in my early twenties. It just became easier to avoid it altogether. Working all these years as a bounty hunter allowed me to focus on work."

"But you're *supposed* to lose yourself. That's what sex is about."

His eyes met mine, and for a moment, I sensed how different he was from other Shifters. It was something I'd noticed my whole life. While Lakota had innate Shifter instincts, he'd also acquired characteristics that were very Chitah-like—the way he would hold a person's gaze and never look away, the intensity of his stare, how quickly he would defend any woman regardless of Breed. Even the way he could intimidate someone with his body language. It was animalistic yet so different from how a wolf behaved.

"Why?" I dared to ask. "What's wrong with touch? What's wrong with feeling good?"

"My mother told me something years ago that—" He grimaced and lowered his head, his hair shielding his face.

I rested my hand on his shoulder. It seemed to give him permission to go on, but he never looked up.

"Do you know about my adoption?" he asked.

"Not really. I figured maybe your mom was too young."

I had come up with a few theories as to why a Shifter would have given up her baby, but none were as simple as a young woman who just wasn't ready for motherhood.

"A man raped my mother," he confessed. "It was someone she trusted—the beta in the pack. That's why I'm here, walking this earth. People say a child is a blessing, but that would mean celebrating my mother's rape."

"I'm sorry," I whispered against his shoulder. "But what does that have to do with dating women?"

He propped his elbows on his knees and looked straight ahead. "A good man raised me, but my true father is a rapist.

His is the blood that courses in my veins. His are the eyes that look upon women with lust."

Then it dawned on me. Lakota had spent most of his adult life believing that he was capable of the barbaric crime his father had committed—that his blood was cursed and would dictate the kind of man he was destined to become, regardless of what values he was raised with. I could only imagine how difficult it must have been when women were suddenly tempting him. He must have rejected them out of fear—fear that he might lose control and hurt them.

"You're not your father," I said firmly. "You can't deny yourself pleasure because of something your father did. There's no sleeping demon inside you that's going to suddenly wake up and change the kind of man you are. Not unless you want it to, and that's always a choice." With the crook of my finger, I turned his chin and forced him to look at me. "My father was a sex and drug addict for a long time. It's no secret. Does that mean it's my destiny too? Does that mean his demons will become mine because we share the same blood?"

"You're not like that," he growled.

I stroked his jaw with the tips of my fingers. "And neither are you. I'll prove it."

He huffed. "How?"

"Sleep with me."

He blinked in surprise, and a flame touched his cheeks.

"I'm not asking for sex, Lakota. I'm asking you to sleep with me."

I held his gaze. Maybe the fates wanted me to heal him. If Lakota didn't overcome his fear, it would hold him back when searching for an alpha to work under. Any decent Packmaster would be apprehensive of selecting a beta who was afraid of women and, more importantly, afraid of what he might do to them.

"You can't keep running from this," I continued, telling him what he already knew. "Lie next to me while I sleep. By morning, you'll know what kind of man you are."

"I can't," he croaked, attempting to stand.

Gripping his shoulder, I held him down. "You will. Those men outside might come back, and who will protect me?"

That little song was for his wolf. Shifters instinctually responded to threats, and he needed a little coaxing. The men outside posed no threat to me any more than the man inside, but they were a good enough reason for him to stay.

Lakota drew in a deep breath, one of resolve. He finally turned and centered his eyes on mine. "I'll stay."

CHAPTER 7

SOMETHING HARD AND WARM PRESSED against my back, startling me out of sleep. I blinked a few times, focusing on the wall beside the bed. Everything was fuzzy in those waking moments. Dim morning light filtered in from behind me, and a wonderful smell filled my nose.

Where am I? Oh yeah, a motel.

I recalled my brief encounter with food poisoning, coming to the motel, taking a shower, Lakota bringing me food, the nightmare, and... *oh holy hell.*

The kiss.

My body tingled just thinking about it. I stretched, then it hit me like a sledgehammer what that rumbling was against my back. It wasn't a dream or even a pillow. It was Lakota Cross, and he had me in a firm grip.

I glanced down at a tangle of arms and couldn't tell where mine ended and his began. We looked like a human pretzel. Lakota was spooning me from behind, his bare chest pressed against my back, his face nuzzled against my nape—and I only knew that because I could feel the heat of his breath in a steady rhythm. Every breath he took seemed to travel all the way down to my core. My bottom was snug against his groin, another unexpected discovery.

Lakota had come into my bed the previous night with great reluctance. He'd clung to the edge of the mattress on the other side as if it were a lifeboat. Eventually he rolled onto his back, hands locked behind his head as his gaze drifted to the ceiling.

He assumed I'd fallen asleep, but sleeping would have been an exercise in futility. Eventually I stopped rolling around and altered my breathing so he would at least think I'd drifted off. Through my tangled hair, I watched him— the way his chest rose and fell with each breath, the way he would simultaneously frown and purse his lips when deep in thought, the way he periodically turned his head to watch me. I would quickly shut my eyes until I heard the soft rustle of his head shifting away. We played that game for what seemed like an hour, and Lakota kept his hands locked behind his head the entire time. After a while, my eyelids grew heavy, and the sound of gentle rain outside lulled me to sleep.

Now a man with the body of a warrior was holding me tight as if I mattered. I had no recollection of wandering hands during the night. His arms felt like iron, and they held me protectively. Everything about the moment was so tender and affectionate that I didn't want to move, afraid that one cough or shift of my body would cause him to sever contact. *Would he recoil? Run away? Roll me over and bury me under his weight?*

I wasn't sure which option was the best one, and that left me even more confused. Only two men had ever held me in their arms when falling asleep, and by morning, they were on their side and I was on mine.

Never had I woken up feeling so safe and protected. I wasn't foolish enough to believe it meant anything. Lakota was undoubtedly craving the feel of being close to another wolf. He'd never really experienced pack life on a daily basis, and I wondered what that kind of separation would do to a wolf. I felt lonely being away from my pack, but at least I had Hope to keep me company. Sometimes our wolves would curl up together, fulfilling that need to bond with other wolves.

But Lakota lived and worked alone. Our connection would probably scare him enough to leap out of bed and hit the road.

"Morning, Freckles," he murmured.

I pretended to be asleep.

He called my bluff. "Can't fool me. Your heart's beating faster, and you stopped snoring."

"I don't snore."

"Of course not. You breathe with gusto."

I turned my head. "I don't like that name. Freckles, I mean."

"I do," he said with a throaty growl.

When his arms relaxed, I rolled over to face him. "You were always good at teasing me," I said, a smile on my lips.

He looked at me lazily, his voice a silken caress across my skin. "I like your freckles."

I liked the way I felt in his arms, but I kept that to myself. "Did you learn something last night?"

His lips eased into a grin. "That you snore like a little mouse."

I poked his chest. "I don't snore. I'm serious. Here I am, in my bra and panties, and all you did was hold me in your arms. Not only that, but I had my back turned to you while in bed. I was vulnerable, and you're more powerful than I am. I hope this convinces you that you've been wrong about yourself this whole time."

"Maybe it's because I know you."

"If you had it in you, it wouldn't matter. In fact, you might feel more entitled, probably the way your father did about your mother since he was the beta in the pack. Don't you feel differently about yourself?"

He nodded slowly. Lakota was still struggling with coming to terms with his true nature, but there was something in his expression I hadn't seen the night before—relief.

"Just promise me something," I said.

"What's that?"

"Promise me you won't keep running from sex."

His blue eyes twinkled. "I've never met a female like you before."

Female. Sometimes he used that word interchangeably with *woman.* Chitahs often used it as a term of endearment. It wasn't something I was used to hearing, but I liked it every time he said it.

"I'm serious, Lakota. I don't want it to hold you back. Promise me the next time you meet someone, you won't hold back."

"Does that include maid service?"

I gave him a look of reproach.

His eyebrows drew together, and he pressed his forehead against mine. "You have my word. The next woman who makes my heart beat fast, I'll invite her to my bed."

I began to regret pushing him, but it was the right thing to do. Wolves in a pack could smell an Achilles' heel, and they would challenge him as a second-in-command. Lakota deserved a better future than that.

He drew back and swept my hair away from my face. "Can we talk about something else? We don't have much time left together." His thumb grazed along my cheek before he wrapped his arm around me again. This time there was nothing sexual in his touch. It was friendly and tender.

I wanted to tell him to keep holding me like that. Once we let go and got out of that bed, we might not see each other again for a long time. We would go back to being friends who ran into each other at the occasional peace party whenever he came into town. Why that mattered, I wasn't sure.

"Jelly sandwiches for breakfast?" I asked.

When he smiled, his eyes crinkled at the corners. "Something better."

And with that, our tender moment crumbled away as he rolled over and sat up. The paper bag rustled, then Lakota held out something for me—a package of cinnamon donuts.

"I remember you buying these once when I drove you and Hope to the gas station to buy ice cream."

Once? He remembers something I ate once *a million years ago?* And the crazy thing was I couldn't even remember the last time I'd eaten those donuts.

I placed the package on my chest and ripped it open, crumbs scattering as I shoved one into my mouth. They were a little stale, but he'd probably picked up the groceries at a nearby convenience store.

Lakota stood up, his jeans unbuttoned but the zipper still fastened. He moseyed into the bathroom and turned on the shower. Meanwhile, I continued eating donuts and pondered how I was going to win over Shikoba.

The water shut off sooner than I'd expected. Lakota sauntered into the room in his jeans, his chest glistening. He hadn't bothered to dry off, and his hair was dripping wet.

"What are you thinking?" I asked around a mouthful of donut.

He lifted his white T-shirt off the floor and put it on. It fit snugly and clung to his body as it soaked up the water. "I'm wondering if we're going to argue this morning."

"Over what?"

He flipped his hair out from inside the collar. "I think we both know."

Maybe it wasn't worth bringing up. I had no intention of leaving until I spoke with Shikoba one last time, and Lakota knew there was no way he could stop me. That didn't mean he wasn't going to try.

When he turned a sharp eye toward my donuts, I became self-conscious about the mess I'd made. Then again, maybe he was taking another gander at how I didn't quite measure up in the breast department. They looked even flatter when I was lying down.

"Let me have one of those," he said.

I felt my cheeks flush, confused for only a nanosecond that he was asking for a donut. Lakota rounded the bed, shoved a donut into his mouth, and turned his attention to a rather uninspiring painting on the wall of a deer standing in the woods.

"Why do you care so much about my sex life?" he asked, still positioned with his back to me.

Setting the donuts aside, I sat up. "Well, you cared enough to share it with me. I don't know. It's something everyone should experience, and the reasons you chose for avoiding it aren't worthy of you."

Lakota's jaw kept working on that donut as he stared at the painting. I wondered if I should shower, but part of me didn't want to if that meant washing away his smell.

And wasn't that a silly thought?

Maybe my uncle William was right. Being away from a pack too long could put some crazy ideas into a woman's head, and here I was, giving sex advice to my best friend's brother. What would Hope think if she knew how quickly I'd lured her brother into my bed? Given that she never dated, she would probably think I was a slut.

And as I sat there in silence, I realized that was what Lakota must think of me as well. Jericho's little girl grew up to be exactly like the man her daddy once was. And even though Lakota and I hadn't done anything sexual, would I have said no if that offer had been on the table? Probably not.

I jolted out of bed and yanked on my jeans.

"What's wrong?" he asked as I shot past him.

"Nothing."

He gripped my arm. "No, not nothing."

I wrenched away and hurried into the bathroom. After sliding on my tank top, I began brushing my teeth.

Lakota filled the doorway behind me, hands gripping the frame above his head. I glanced at him in the mirror while I brushed my molars.

"You're the first person I've ever slept with," he quipped.

I rinsed my mouth out. "Was it as good for you as it was for me?"

His jaw set. "Who are these men you've slept with? Do I know any of them?"

Was he trying to start something with me so I would get mad enough to leave town? I ignored him and put on my turquoise necklace.

His hands lowered so he was holding the frame on either side. "Are you seeing anyone now?"

I took my clean panties from the towel rack and stuffed them into my purse, leaving the toothbrush and toothpaste behind since they were travel size and not mine. "Move. I need to leave."

"Not until you tell me what's wrong."

Flustered, I adjusted my purse strap. "Maybe you should ignore everything I've told you about relationships. I can't tell you how to live your life. Women are complicated, and if you can't handle a mood swing, maybe adding sex to the equation is doing more harm than good. I just... I didn't want you to go around thinking that you were broken."

I immediately wanted to retract my words. "Broken" was too harsh, but that had been exactly the look shadowing his expression when he bared his soul about his real father. That knowledge *had* broken him—stripped away the promising future he had as a man, a Shifter, and a lover.

Tainted it.

I couldn't even look him in the eye. As lovely as the previous night had been for me, it was probably terrifying for him. Or embarrassing. I'd behaved like some kind of half-naked temptress, hoping to slap a Band-Aid on a problem that was probably bigger than I could comprehend, a dark truth that had cast a shadow on his entire life.

When he reached out to touch my face, I shrank back.

His brows knitted. "What changed between us?"

"There is no us. There's just you and me living separate lives. We both took a detour, but I need to get back on the road. I have to go."

He stepped aside to let me out. "Afraid a wolf will tie you down and make you quit all your big dreams?"

I shouldered past him.

"That's it, isn't it?" he asked. "Casual sex is fine because no strings are attached. You're afraid to mate."

I impulsively hurled a pillow at his face. With lightning-fast reflexes, he knocked it away.

"That's not who I am!"

He folded his arms across his chest. "Then how come Hope never mentioned that you had a steady boyfriend? If a wolf doesn't put a claim on you, sex is casual. I thought *they* were the ones who didn't want to get serious, but maybe I was wrong."

"You just know everything, don't you?"

He leaned against the wall, his hands tucked beneath his biceps, pushing them out. "Maybe."

With a heavy heart, I gave the room a final inspection and took a deep breath. Sometimes I had a fiery temper, so I gathered my emotions and smothered them before I said something I would regret. "Let's not go away mad at each other. Can we pretend this never happened? I love Hope too much to have friction going on in the background every time we have a get-together." I approached him but kept my distance. "You don't want a relationship with me. I'm so sorry for meddling in your personal life the way I did, but you opened up to me with that secret, and I felt like I had to do something or say something about it. I don't want to fix you, and I don't want you to fix me. I'm not perfect by a long shot. We're just two old friends who got caught in a rainstorm and sought shelter under the same tree. Or in this case, a bed." I gestured behind me, then slapped my hand against my hip. "The storm's passed, Lakota."

An almost imperceptible smile touched Lakota's lips. He tilted his head to the side, his voice just as soft as the look he was giving me. "You're poetic."

I bit my lip and held on to my purse strap as if it were a

lifeline. "Next time you're in town, we'll go out and grab some barbecue."

He lifted his chin. "I can do you one better. We'll camp out like old times."

I chuckled. "In your father's backyard?"

"Promise you'll come?"

The tension between us melted away, and I gave him a wistful smile. As much as I would have liked to roll back the years, we'd changed. "I've got a business to run now. Not as much time on my hands, so we'll see."

"You can always hire help. How about Wheeler?"

A laugh bubbled out, and I covered my mouth. "Are you trying to kill my business before it even gets off the ground? He's great with numbers, but if you put him behind a cash register, he would fill up a swear jar, not a tip jar."

Lakota pressed a chaste kiss to my forehead, and my heart clenched. "Take care of yourself, Freckles."

This was goodbye. We led separate lives, and that meant we might not see each other again for months, maybe years. Suddenly there seemed no appropriate way to say farewell. This was new territory—a night I would press into my heart. It would rank with some of the greatest moments in my life, and it was special because it was ours alone. I hoped he wouldn't become resentful toward me for thinking I could cure his lifelong trauma in one night, but that was always a possibility.

Uncertain what to say, I did the only thing that came naturally. I curled into his warm embrace and hugged him goodbye.

CHAPTER 8

L AKOTA WAITED IMPATIENTLY OUTSIDE THE motel, his arms warming in the sun and his T-shirt now dry. After their embrace, Lakota had been the one to leave the room, and Melody hadn't come out since. She'd probably changed her mind about a shower, or maybe she was practicing avoidance since he hadn't budged from the spot outside her door.

When a horn blared, he stood up from the walkway and waved at Tak, who suddenly hit the gas and made the black pickup lurch forward.

Lakota had been sent here on a job, and he'd learned rather quickly how difficult it would be to acclimate. He'd met Tak in a bar one night when Tak hustled him in a game of pool, only to find out that Lakota was a better hustler. Lakota offered to buy him a beer, but Tak wanted tea instead. They had a good conversation and hit it off. It was a good thing too—Tak was a big guy who could have been a Viking in a past life. Lakota needed to immerse himself in the community, and Tak was his way in. The local Shifters were standoffish, and it hadn't taken long for him to see the division between the packs and the tribes.

Tak rolled down the window and stuck his head out. "I could get used to this ride," he said, a robust laugh setting off his remark. "She's small, but she's got spirit."

Feigning annoyance, Lakota slowed his pace and folded his arms. Despite Tak's brutish appearance and the ink on the left side of his face, the man carried a sense of humor that his father frowned upon. Understandable. His father just so happened to be Shikoba, the chief, and he probably didn't think his people would respect an alpha who was always hamming it up. Lakota noticed how the tribe looked at Tak differently, but he wasn't entirely sure it had to do with his friend's personality traits. His alpha power wasn't weak—that was for certain. It practically vibrated lampshades whenever he entered a room. But Lakota couldn't pry too much into Tak's personal affairs, not if it meant jeopardizing their friendship. He'd worked hard to get in good with the pack, and he needed to solve his case.

Lakota tried like hell not to look back at the motel room to see whether the curtains were still drawn or if Melody was watching him leave. The way they'd left it, he didn't know what to think. He'd spent the past fifteen minutes debating on going back inside and throwing caution to the wind, but she was right. He had a job to do, and this was neither the time nor the place—especially not if it meant putting her in danger.

The passenger door squealed when he opened it and hopped in.

Tak leaned toward Lakota and pulled the air to his face with a cupped hand. His eyes closed. "Do you smell that?"

Lakota slammed the door. "Smell what?"

"A woman." He patted Lakota on the chest and belted out a laugh.

Lakota knocked his arm away and called him a donkey in his native tongue. When he glanced up, his breath hitched. Melody was standing in the open doorway, and by the looks of it, she hadn't showered. Her hair was dry, and the wind picked it up while she dug around in her big purse. She looked stunning in those jeans. Everything she made was an extension of her personality, and he immediately regretted not having said something about them. It wasn't just the patchwork that caught his eye. It was the way the fabric wrapped around her slim legs, showing off the curve of her ass.

Though Lakota might be a virgin, he wasn't a blind man. Melody wasn't as voluptuous as some women, yet her body was undeniably feminine and graceful—a narrow waist, long legs, a round ass that could turn any wolf's head, and delicate breasts that she didn't seem to appreciate half as much as he did.

Tak snapped his fingers in front of Lakota's face. "She bewitched you."

Lakota yawned. "Not my type."

"Sure," Tak said, putting the truck in reverse. "Your Native heart says no, but your blue eyes are traitors."

Just as Tak turned the truck around, Lakota glimpsed Melody heading toward the vending machines. She wasn't going to give up and go home. That much he knew. Hope's first meeting hadn't gone well, and he could tell by her enthusiastic tone that she was placing all bets on Melody to secure a deal. "I would be so fortunate to work with Shikoba," she'd said. "No one sells stones as beautiful as his."

And she was right. Shikoba employed his packmates as traders, working with tribes around the country to acquire the finest quality gemstones. Those he purchased from were exclusively Breed, and as far as Lakota knew, he only did business with the tribes.

"You're quiet this morning," Tak noted.

Lakota rubbed his eye with the heel of his hand. "Where are we going?"

"I'd take you back to your place, but since I'm driving your truck, I wouldn't have a way home. So consider this a kidnapping."

"Maybe we should pull over and get breakfast before my abduction," he suggested, hoping to avoid running into Melody again.

Tak jerked the wheel, gunning past a small Toyota that

was sputtering down the lane. "Since when do you dine out? Or is that the white man talking?"

Lakota playfully punched him in the arm. Tak was the only one who didn't seem bothered by Lakota being biracial. Everyone else, including Shikoba, had accepted Lakota as a friend of the tribe, but he wasn't oblivious to their beliefs. It was one reason he hadn't revealed the whole truth—that his mother wasn't even full-blooded. She was half, which made him a quarter. But what little ancestral blood ran through him was enough, and aside from his eyes, no one could mistake which were the dominant genes.

Tak cleared his throat. "Did anyone see you with her? You should have stayed in your motel room and left her alone. Temptation only brings trouble."

"She won't be here for long."

Glaring at him, Tak said, "You think that matters to the wolves in this town? All they see is a white woman and a brown man."

"You think I care what those jokers think?"

Tak shrugged and began whistling a tune.

Most of Lakota's jobs involved hunting and capturing declared outlaws, but he was on a special assignment. He'd heard rumors about murders near tribal land in Oklahoma, so when the higher authority had tapped him on the shoulder and asked him to sniff out the killer, he didn't hesitate. They gave him an advance and agreed to pay him the remainder whether he caught the killer or not, just so long as he provided them with new information. What made the murders especially concerning was that the human police had discovered them. Since the victims had been Shifters, each discovery increased the odds of humans finding out about Breed. The higher authority continually intervened by altering files, halting autopsies, and scrubbing memories of those who were on the crime scene, but unfortunately, the media involvement made it increasingly difficult to keep it a secret. Lakota's job was to uncover the truth, and until he found the killer, Melody was in just as much danger as any of the locals.

Lakota rolled his window down and rested his arm on the door. The wind was cooler, the sky seemed bluer, the trees greener, the air cleaner.

Tak messed around with the radio stations before putting on a pair of black shades. The drums and the electric guitar synced into a relentless pounding that filled the cab. Tak liked all that hard rock and metal, but it wasn't to Lakota's taste.

Lakota's thoughts drifted to the night before. *Why did I reveal such a shameful part of my life to Melody?* The truth had flown out of his mouth before he knew what was happening, and in that moment, it seemed important that she know—not just the truth about his virginity but also the reason behind it. Instead of laughing, she'd listened. He'd never told anyone about how his mother's rape had affected him, had changed the way he saw his place in the world.

Illegitimate.

A burden.

A sin.

He had always accepted his adoption and loved both families without question. Though he hadn't always known the reason behind his unusual family situation, his birth mother had promised him that one day when he was a man, she would tell him the full story. That day marked the end of his innocence.

Lakota sighed. *The shame.*

That he was the result of a man assaulting his mother consumed him like nothing else. How could he ever give his heart to a woman, knowing that a rapist's blood coursed through his veins?

That man was long gone, and Lakota had found a way to channel his rage into something positive with his job. Hunting outlaws took the edge off, but he still kept his distance from women. People often remarked on personality traits he shared with his mother. So he often wondered what he shared with his father. Deep down, Lakota never felt like he was capable of hurting a woman. But he was still afraid that if he didn't learn to control his desires, he just might. That was what shame did to a man.

The previous night was the first time he hadn't felt suffocated by the heavy burden of guilt and fear, and Melody had freely given him that gift. His wolf wanted nothing more than to protect her. In one night, she had shown him what no one else could.

"You're far away," Tak said. "Must be a nice place. But whenever you decide to come back to the land of the living, we need to talk."

Lakota frowned. "About what?"

"Koi's gone missing."

"Maybe he's still hunting."

Tak cut him a sharp glare. "Koi never stays out overnight. When he didn't come home yesterday morning, it had a few people talking. No one's heard from him, and his mother's upset. She thinks the storm bringing that woman was a bad omen."

Lakota rolled up his window so he wouldn't have the wind blasting in his ear. "Did they send out a search party? He probably took shelter in a cave. A few good wolves could probably sniff him out."

"That's what my father will decide," Tak said flatly. "The elders are smoking their pipes and probably trying to conjure spirits or something. Thought I'd let you know before we get there. Kaota is on the warpath."

Kaota was Koi's older half brother—much older. Lakota didn't know the full story, only that they shared the same father. The two couldn't be more different. Kaota was stern with hard features, whereas Koi was a young man with an adventurous heart.

When they finally reached the property, some of the tribe had shifted. Three brown wolves darted across their path and disappeared into the trees.

"No one picked up his scent?" Lakota asked.

"Nothing for you to worry about. You can go home from here. Too much drama." The truck shook when it hit a steep hole as they circled in front of the house. "Someone needs to fill that hole," Tak grumbled. "That wildflower of yours tripped over it."

Lakota scrubbed a hand over his face just remembering it. When Melody had emerged from the house, he could tell straight away that something wasn't right. Her eyes were glazed over and skin ashen. It was pure torture having to stand there and pretend he didn't give a shit after seeing her fall flat on her face. He'd known her forever, and his wolf thrashed within him, bringing him precariously close to shifting.

Burying his thoughts, Lakota hopped out of the truck. The minute his shoes hit the gravel, one of the little ones in the tribe came bounding toward him. She was three and fearless. Tak was one of her favorites, but she adored Lakota's blue eyes.

He lifted her up and swung her in his arms. *"How's my little warrior?"* he boomed.

She giggled, her dark eyes wide and full of sparkle. "Sky! Sky!" she said, touching her hand to his forehead. "Bwoo." She meant to say *blue*, but she was struggling with the English language since the children learned their native tongue first.

"That's right, kiddo," he said. "Blue. Like the sky." He pointed up and she gaped, mesmerized by the near-perfect match to his eyes.

Near the house, the women were speaking in a tight huddle, consoling Koi's distraught mother. Koi might have run away or gotten into a tangle with a rogue, but something about this disappearance didn't feel right.

Lakota set the child down and approached Tak, his voice low. "Keep me updated. I'll see if anyone in the territory is talking about it."

Tak flashed a smile. "Sure you aren't sneaking back to the motel?"

Lakota's heart rocketed in his chest when cries erupted from inside the house. Tak charged through the door, Lakota close behind. The sounds of wails and shouts came from the rec room. A cluster of men gathered around a television, their faces a combination of anger, shock, and grief. Three of them tucked the women protectively against them and led them out of the room.

"Keep her out!" someone bellowed.

Lakota steered his attention to the television. A female reporter in a silk blouse was live on the scene where a body had been found. Fragmented shots of police lights flashing on a car, crime-scene tape, and officers standing behind a barricade near a private road were spliced together. When she revealed the victim was an unidentified woman, Lakota gave Tak a puzzled look.

"Sources say the body was discovered by two hikers, but cause of death has not yet been confirmed," the reporter went on. "Authorities haven't released the identity of the victim, but she's described as a young Caucasian female. No word on whether or not this is related to the string of unsolved murders occurring in the area since last November. Local residents are shaken and worried who might be next... and when."

"Any information on the wolf?" the man in the studio asked.

Lakota held his breath.

"No, Steve. Officers aren't commenting on the wolf found on the scene. An animal attack seems probable, but they're not yet ruling out foul play."

As they wrapped up the report, a live chopper view of a clearing in the woods came on the screen. Someone was dragging a wolf by the hind legs toward a truck.

More cries sounded, and shouts of outrage filled the room. One man turned away from the screen and slammed his eyes shut. It was Koi's wolf. The markings on his tail and legs were unmistakable.

Moments later, the lament of a heartbroken mother ripped through the house and shook everyone to the core.

Tak's eyes glittered with tears, and he turned to face Lakota. "What will they do with his body?"

"Probably animal services," Lakota said, not mentioning that they would conduct an autopsy on the animal to find out the cause of death and whether or not it had rabies. That meant removing the head and shipping it to a laboratory for further testing. Likely, they would incinerate the remains.

The careless disregard for Koi's body sickened Lakota, and he knew he had to get that wolf out of human hands and bring him home, not just for the sake of protecting Breed secrets but also for honor. Every wolf deserved a proper burial.

CHAPTER 9

A S I NEARED THE TURNOFF to Shikoba's land, a black
truck rocketed toward me, the engine roaring. When
it flew by at an illegal speed, the rush of air whipped
my hair in front of my face.

"Kill me, why don't you!" I shouted out the window.
"Idiot."

Probably drunk too. Country people didn't take speed
limits seriously. If he had run me off the road and knocked
me unconscious, I would have been in bad shape. There wasn't
exactly an alpha around to coax me awake and force me to
shift. I cranked up Engelbert Humperdinck to get my mind
off of hurtling into a tree at sixty miles per hour.

"What the—"

Two wolves scurried across the road. I slowed down,
careful not to accidentally hit one of them. While I'd grown
up on the outskirts of Austin, my pack had always preferred
shifting at night. It was safer, and our wolves knew better
than to go near the main road—too many opportunities for
humans to spot us, and someone might have half a mind to
pull out their shotgun.

I neared Shikoba's house, but unlike the previous day,
the front yard was empty. I switched off the music since my
windows were down.

"Here goes nothing." I grabbed my purse and exited the vehicle.

The sun kissed my bare shoulders and promised a warm day. A wasp buzzed past me before disappearing into the woods. Nearing the house, I noticed how eerily silent it was. In a pack that large, noise was always going on somewhere.

"Hello?" I knocked on the front door, then turned to look at the property. Wolves running loose made me especially nervous.

When the door opened, a young boy around the age of twelve or thirteen greeted me.

"Hi, I'm here to speak with Shikoba."

He glanced over his shoulder, a look of uncertainty on his face.

"It's business," I continued. "I was here yesterday. Do you think you could find him for me or get your mom?"

As soon as I mentioned his mother, he stood up a little taller and lifted his chin. I'd seen that look before. Boys that age didn't like people seeing them as little kids who couldn't make a simple decision. Without a word, he gestured for me to follow him.

The main room was empty, and I wondered if maybe they were all out hunting or fishing. He led me to a small room devoid of windows. After switching on a floor lamp, he shut the door and left me alone.

I turned in a circle, admiring the paintings of warriors on horseback and wolves on the hunt. Two wooden chairs faced each other in front of an unlit fireplace, but I chose to stand and look at the pottery on a handcrafted shelf against the right-hand wall. Some pieces were cracked and weathered, still holding on to their charm, while others were new, celebrating a proud young generation honoring the old ways. I flipped a switch on the wall, and lights illuminated each shelf, highlighting the hundreds if not thousands of years of the tribe's history.

When my legs grew weary of standing, I took a seat in

one of the chairs and daydreamed about Moonglow. I pushed aside all the worries and imagined a successful future—finally becoming a woman my family could be proud of. That wasn't to say they weren't proud of me already, but I had no accomplishments beneath my belt aside from a home-based business. Maybe having a famous father had lit a fire under me to do my own thing.

I worried my lip and thought about what Lakota had said about my pushing men away and not getting serious because it might interfere with my plans. He was right, but that didn't necessarily mean it was wrong. Most young men wanted to find a mate and start a family, and none had ever given me reassurance that they would let their mate pursue all her passions first. It always had to be a choice, a competition of which was more important—dreams or family. If I couldn't find a man who understood that they were one and the same, then I was better off alone.

After what seemed like an hour, I finally heard some commotion in the adjacent room. Curious, I cracked open the door and peered out.

"One is enough," a man growled, a dagger in his grip. "How many brothers are you willing to lose before you take a stand?"

The tattooed man from the day before stepped forward. "And how many of your brothers are you willing to sacrifice to make a point? That's not our way. We don't have all the facts—"

"To hell with the facts! Why are you so eager to sit back and do nothing, Tak?"

Maybe I need to ease on out of here. It looked like the pack was embroiled in a family dispute, and I didn't have any desire to be around a pack of angry wolves. Shikoba could wait, and maybe Hope could call him later and smooth things over. The way the man in the next room was slicing his dagger and spewing curses was all I needed to make my decision.

As I slipped out the door and crept along the wall, the chatter died.

Completely.

It was so quiet that the board creaking beneath the weight of my foot sounded like falling timber. My heart galloped when every last man in that room had his eyes on me.

"Who let in the white woman?" the man with the knife spat.

The one called Tak replied, "Shikoba's doing business with her."

"Don't play me for a fool. She left yesterday with her tail between her legs." Before I knew it, the man crossed in front of me and blocked my exit. He pinned me with a hostile glare, making the hair on my arms stand up.

Tak raised his voice. "Let her go, Kaota. She's not our concern."

Kaota gripped my arm painfully. I tried to wrench away, but his hold was iron. "Our trouble started yesterday with her arrival. She's a dark cloud and brought death to our people." He nodded at two men, who then hurried out the front door. A few of the others looked torn but didn't interfere.

We were standing halfway in the main room, a circle of about ten people around us—mostly men. No one stepped forward to help, and that sent panic racing up my spine.

"I was leaving," I said, my voice steady and calm. "Shikoba wasn't expecting me, and it looks like I've come at a bad time. I didn't mean to interrupt, so I'll just go and let you get back to your meeting."

I twisted my arm, but Kaota's large hand wrapped all the way around it, making it impossible to break free. Without the Packmaster present and not knowing who was second-in-command, I needed to remain calm and not instigate anything. If the local Council had no authority over them, then that meant they followed their own rules.

Tak stepped forward and leveled Kaota with one look. "Let the woman go," he said slowly, dangerously.

A wave of energy rippled in the air, and in that moment, I realized Tak was an alpha wolf. Aside from children, packs didn't have more than one alpha. Then again, it was more of a tribe than a pack. At least the alpha was on my side.

For now.

Kaota reluctantly let go, and the two men stared each other down. Before anyone changed their mind, I fled out the front door, my arm still sore from Kaota's grip.

When I reached the bottom of the steps, I skidded to a halt. "Hey, those are mine!"

Kaota's buddies were stalking away from my Jeep, one of them holding my quiver and bow over his head to show the others.

"*You bring weapons onto our land?*" Kaota bellowed. He marched down the steps behind me, anger flickering in his eyes.

For a moment, I thought about running to the car and leaving. But that quiver was sentimental—my aunt had given it to me.

Tak cut between us and faced his packmate, his arms outstretched. "Ease up, Kaota. She didn't bring them into the house. We're all hurting here, but she has nothing to do with this. An angry warrior never hits his intended target. What kind of man takes his anger out on a woman? That's not our way."

"According to the news, it is," Kaota retorted. "How long do you think it will take for the local packs to figure out that the wolf was Koi? They know our wolves by sight. They're going to point the finger at us for killing that woman."

"On what proof?" Tak countered.

Teeth clenched, Kaota walked forward. "They're looking for someone to blame for those murders."

"What if it *was* Koi?" someone asked.

Kaota exploded into action, shifting into a brown wolf and lunging at the man who'd raised the question. He also shifted, and a fight ensued. They rose up on their hind legs, teeth gnashing, viciously barking and growling as blood stained their fur and the gravel below. I clenched the strap of my purse.

Tak charged into the fray and grabbed Kaota's wolf around the neck, holding him in a viselike grip. "Enough!"

Energy crackled in the air, and I stayed catatonic. My wolf was pacing nervously beneath my skin. She had never fought another wolf, and though I knew she was a tough girl, a pack stood together.

And this wasn't my pack.

Several wolves emerged from the woods. I counted six, including the two in the skirmish. No women were present except for one or two on the upper balcony.

My throat went dry, and I was breathing hard as if I'd run a mile. The only one who could have protected me was engaged with one of the wolves, trying to pin him down.

"Shift," Tak demanded.

In the blink of an eye, the brown wolf shifted back to a man. Kaota, now unclothed, peeled back his lips. "I want blood. I want revenge for my brother! Koi deserved an honorable death."

A loud motor steered everyone's attention away as a black truck approached, Lakota behind the wheel. He glanced at me briefly, his expression tight.

The hairs on my neck stood up when a woman on the balcony wailed, and I saw the others shielding their eyes, crestfallen. *What about Lakota's appearance could have elicited such a reaction?*

Confused, I watched as one of the men approached the truck and peered into the bed. Then he cried out, speaking in a language I didn't understand.

Lakota shut off the engine as the men gathered around the bed of the truck, lowering the tailgate and speaking in low murmurs. Kaota branched away from the group, a dead wolf in his arms and tears staining his cheeks.

I felt a catch in my throat when an older woman hurried

down the steps, her arms outstretched and her spirit broken. She sang, her words nothing but raw emotion, and fell to her knees. I didn't need to speak her language to know that she was the wolf's mother. Tak helped her up, keeping her steady as the men reverently carried their fallen brother. Everyone laid their hands on the wolf and chanted words of prayer. I watched helplessly as the mother cradled the wolf's head and cleansed him with her tears, repeating his name mixed with what I guessed were words that only a mother could give.

They carried him inside, and some followed but not all. A few of the men were livid and beyond consolation. In a pack, it didn't matter if you were related by blood. All were brothers.

Lakota stalked toward me, his voice low. "I told you not to come."

"I was leaving, but—"

He spun around and punched a wolf that had lunged for me. The animal flipped over, and when he finally staggered to his feet, he trotted toward the house.

Lakota curved his arm protectively in front of me, forcing me to stand behind him. "Shikoba!" he called out. "Shikoba!"

The leader of the Iwa tribe appeared in the doorway and descended the steps. He came close enough but kept a measure of distance between us.

"I'm sorry for your loss, but you have a problem," Lakota began. "The local packs are surrounding your land. I barely made it through the entrance to your property."

Though I stepped aside to watch them talk, Lakota kept his eye on me.

Shikoba shook his head, his eyes woeful. "I knew one day it would come to this."

Lakota gestured at me. "Send this woman away so we can discuss the details. There are too many angry wolves, and they can scent she's not part of the pack. You have a son to bury, so I won't take up much of your time."

"Give her back her weapons," Tak snarled.

The man tossed my quiver to the ground and then

snapped my recurve bow over his knee, splitting the wood clean through.

My heart shattered.

I'd had that bow since I first learned how to shoot with it. The memories of practicing with my grandmother, the hunting trips with my uncle Reno, the words of wisdom from my father on owning a weapon responsibly, the respect from my Packmaster when he saw me as a strong warrior—gone. My lip quivered, and I fought back the hot tears as I knelt down and gathered my arrows that had fallen out of the quiver.

"How did the locals find out the wolf was Koi?" Lakota asked, his voice quieter.

"Many in the community have lived here for centuries. They do not come on tribal land, but they know our wolves." Shikoba's foot scraped against the gravel, and he gave me a fixed stare. "The woman cannot go."

"She *has* to go," Kaota snarled, yanking up his pants. His long hair was unbound, the wind lifting the silken mane. "She doesn't belong here. She's a curse on our people—on our land. You know the old stories about strangers and a storm. They are bringers of death."

Shikoba's voice never faltered. "What would they say if a white woman walked out of here on the same day that one of their own was murdered? They're looking for a reason to take what's ours. We must not give them one."

I stood up with my broken bow and arrows. "I can't stay here. I have to go home."

"You *will* stay," Shikoba said, inviting no argument. "Do you think those men are waiting out there to save you? This is for your protection."

"I'm not from around here. They're not going to stop me from leaving."

Shikoba tapped his cane on the ground. "No matter. Too much anger is poisoning the air. They might turn on you, and I won't have your blood on my hands."

Lakota rubbed his whiskery chin. "I can call the police and report them."

"It's the Council you need to call," Tak informed him. "Not the police. Humans aren't welcome on our land."

"The Council doesn't have the manpower to haul those men away, but the cops do."

Tak folded his arms, his eyebrows drawing together. "Oh? If they're not standing on the property, then they're not trespassing. Cops will wonder what we're hiding, and who knows what an angry mob will tell them. This is a show of intimidation. They're fencing us in so we can't go anywhere."

I clutched Lakota's arm and whispered, "I can't stay. You can't just leave me here."

He whispered back, "If you stay, I stay."

Shikoba noticed our whispering and drew closer.

Lakota quickly turned to the chief and closed the distance between them. "I'll guard the woman and make sure she doesn't run. If someone caught her escaping, it would make the situation look even worse."

Shikoba clapped him on the shoulder. "Very well. I must make preparations for a burial. Come find me in an hour and we'll talk." As he walked toward the door, he raised his voice, addressing his pack. "No more fighting, and anyone who lays a hand on this woman will answer to me. You shame me with your cowardly bickering. You are all brothers."

"You have to let me go," I pleaded to Lakota.

He slowly shook his head and gave me a worried look. "You shouldn't be here. It's a witch hunt."

"How did you recover Koi's body?" Tak asked, closing in on our private circle.

Lakota turned to face him, still using his body to shield me from danger. "I asked the local Council of Shifters to intervene."

Tak threw back his head. "So that's why half the territory is at our doorstep."

"They already knew from the footage on TV, and those who didn't would have found out soon enough."

Tak clapped Lakota on the shoulder. "Thank you for bringing him home, brother. I mean that."

Lakota extended his arm to Tak's shoulder, and they held that position for a moment before Tak turned away to rejoin his family, leaving us alone.

I strode toward my Jeep with my broken bow and tossed the mangled remains into the back seat. "What happened to the wolf?"

Lakota took my quiver and reached through the window, placing it carefully on the seat. "They found a dead girl. She belonged to a local rogue. I don't know what her animal was, but you can bet if she had been in a pack, Shikoba's tribe would be preparing for battle instead of a funeral."

"What does that have to do with the wolf?"

He frowned. "Everyone liked Koi. He was twenty going on fifteen. One of Shikoba's nephews. They found his body near the woman."

I swallowed hard, daring to ask the question. "Did he kill her? Was it a murder-suicide?"

An eagle cried, and the wind whispered as it blew through the treetops. Lakota swept back his hair. It was deep brown with a rich luster, thicker and wilder than those in the Iwa tribe.

"I don't know," he said. "She might have mortally wounded him in self-defense, or maybe someone attacked them both. The tribe will inspect his wounds and try to piece together the facts, but the crime scene is the only place that will tell the whole story." Lakota rubbed his chin and glanced back at the house. "Let's walk."

We sauntered toward the house, and I found myself walking closer to him than I normally would.

"It's getting dangerous," he continued. "From what I gather, there was always friction in the community between the tribe and everyone else. They have a history, and that's how small Shifter towns are. But the recent crimes really set things on fire. They were inexplicable and brutal. It's been a pain in the ass for the higher authority to keep sending out a Vampire to scrub memories and alter documents. They couldn't erase a body, but they made them believe that some were suicide. That's how the news was reporting some of them, but Shifters knew better."

"How?"

He stopped and turned to face me. "Because the women belonged to *them*."

"Meaning the outside packs and rogues, not the tribes." So *that* was why Lakota was undercover. Too many deaths would draw attention—FBI kind of attention. And the murders were all Shifter women who lived in the community.

He scratched the side of his nose. "The locals think the tribe is responsible. Some are calling it human sacrifice, others a crime of passion."

"Passion?"

"A few of the women were rumored to be having secret love affairs with some of the men in the tribe. Since the packs believe we're nothing but savages who can't control our impulses and violent tendencies, it lends belief to their theory."

"Do you think that's true? About the love affairs, I mean."

He shrugged, his eyes swinging skyward. "I don't know. Shikoba's warned his men to stay away, but he does it for the sake of protecting his people from scandal. It's frowned upon, but you can't stop folks from doing what they want in secret. Most of the younger people think differently than their elders."

"Is that why there weren't any women at the bar?"

"I don't know what the outside packs are doing, but you're right. Fewer local women have been going out to the bars—especially where tribes are allowed. I suppose they're either scared or were ordered to stay home and out of trouble."

"But what about Koi? He was a victim. Doesn't that prove the tribes aren't behind these murders?"

He stopped and faced me. "Koi's death links the tribe to the murders, and the local Shifters will draw whatever conclusion they like. You've heard of witch hunts. It still plays out in the media and small towns among humans. Here you've got a bunch of ancients who won't let go of the past. People don't want to accept that one of their own is capable of committing these crimes." Lakota's eyes skated down to my arm, and he gingerly took my elbow. When he noticed the red marks, he glowered. My pulse jumped when I saw dark fury flickering in his eyes. "Who put that mark on you?"

I glanced down at the red marks on my arm, which were threatening to bruise. Knowing Lakota might do something foolish like start a fight, I replied with humor and gently pulled away. "You did. All that spooning last night."

But Lakota wasn't laughing. I'd never seen him look so menacing. "Don't play with me, female. I would never put a mark on you. *Who* did it?"

I centered my eyes on his. "Lakota, I need you right now. You're the only thing standing in the way of those men shifting and tearing me apart. Don't blow your cover because of a bruise. You're the only one who can stop these murders." I worried my lip before giving him what he wanted. "It was Kaota."

He released a controlled breath and briefly touched the ends of my hair before putting distance between us. "Come on, Freckles. Let's go inside."

CHAPTER 10

WHILE SHIKOBA'S FAMILY PREPARED FOR the ceremony, Lakota and I made ourselves scarce. We sat in the kitchen for a spell and talked as if we were strangers, always aware that someone might overhear us. When I noticed the signal on my phone had bars, I excused myself to the bathroom to call Hope.

"Are you surviving up there?" she asked. "I thought you'd be on your way home by now."

"I'm still alive." I put the toilet lid down and took a seat. "It's just taking longer than usual. How did everything go with dealer number two?"

After a pregnant pause, she said, "It fell through. Oh, Mel. Everything's a disaster. I had high hopes for this guy, but I found out he doesn't deal in gemstones I like to use. He was pushing the expensive ones. I don't have any interest in diamonds, emeralds, and rubies. That's not the kind of jewelry I design. What are we going to do? I'll have to cancel all these orders, and no one is going to trust me again. Once my current inventory sells out, there won't be any more income from my end. This is a complete disaster."

Hope was a strong woman, but she also took things to heart. Hearing her on the verge of tears was like a punch to the gut, and I decided to fight harder to fix the situation.

"Are you sure that's all that's bothering you?" I asked.

She sighed. "I had a dream."

"About what?"

"That you were lost in a blizzard. Lakota was there."

"Lakota?"

"Yes, and I don't ever have dreams about my brother. I saw him following bloody tracks in the snow, but I couldn't tell where they led to."

"Well, if you find out, let me know," I said with a laugh. "Sorry, I don't mean to joke around. It was just a dream. You're probably stressing yourself out."

"I'm worried about you."

I leaned forward. "I'm fine, your brother's fine—"

"How would you know if Lakota's fine?"

I bit my lip. "I'm *sure* your brother's fine. I know how you and your mother are about dreams. I'll take care of everything. You hear me? It's going to be fine. *We're* going to be fine. If you get any inquiries on your purchase orders, we won't cancel them. We'll just tell everyone there's a shipping delay. But I promise I'm going to fix this, even if we have to pay someone extra for the short term. It'll work out."

"I hope so. What about Shikoba? You're close to making a deal with him, right? That's why you're still there? Oh, Mel, you have no idea how lucky I'd be to work with him. Everyone respects him, and I'd have guaranteed sales among the tribes with his name attached to my product. My father would be so proud."

And there it was. Hope didn't want to disappoint customers or shine a bad light on our business, but part of it had nothing to do with either of those things. It had to do with her father—showing him that she was responsible, capable, and worthy of his respect. After all, Hope was his only child by blood.

I stood up and leaned against the sink. "Do you think you'll be okay setting up the store by yourself? I'm going to get out of here as soon as I can, but I don't know when that'll be. Today, tomorrow... I'm not sure."

"If it means closing a deal with Shikoba, you can stay for the entire month. I'll have your brothers help me set up the store."

I erupted with laughter and quickly covered my mouth before anyone outside heard. "Just keep them away from the mannequins. They can do a hard day's work, but they're also a bunch of goofballs. Have them transport the inventory out of storage and help with hanging up all the artwork." I tapped my finger against my teeth, trying to think. "Is there anyone in your pack who can help with the displays? I'd rather you not ask my parents, or they'll start wondering why I'm not back yet. I don't want the pack coming up here."

"Oh, no," she quickly agreed. "That would be disastrous. Your pack showing up on tribal land might scare off our only prospect. I'll talk to my mother. She can help around the store, but too much physical work might flare up her bad hip. Do you think Naya would mind pitching in? She's so good with this kind of thing and—"

"We can trust her," I said, already liking the idea. Naya wasn't a snitch and didn't like men trampling all over a woman's right to do things on her own. My family didn't need to know every detail about what was going on in Oklahoma, especially if it could put Lakota in danger.

"Call me if there's anything I can do," she said. "But don't worry about the store. I've got that covered."

She'd put my mind at ease. We couldn't postpone our opening, which meant she would have to do the work of two people to get things in order. But that was Hope, someone I could always count on. "You're the best, you know that?"

"Spread the rumor," she quipped.

"Hope?"

"Yes?"

"Um, how did the windows look this morning?"

"Sparkling. Call me if you need anything."

I had a feeling that Hope was being just as evasive and supportive as I was. Hopefully the graffiti someone had left was a onetime deal, but it made me uncomfortable at the thought of leaving her alone. At least Lennon and Hendrix would be there to look out for her.

When I ended the call, my heart sank. I didn't have the courage to tell her that Shikoba was never going to lock in a deal with us, and that made me feel twice as guilty for all the hard work she was doing. But Hope needed to focus on the store and remain positive. She had a tendency to let misfortune get the best of her. If I had to call her former dealer and pay him what he wanted for the final shipment, then so be it. Surely there had to be someone else out there who dealt with Shifters.

A knock sounded at the door, and before I could turn, it opened.

Lakota came in and sat down on the edge of the tub in front of me. "Everyone's outside setting up. The elders are gathered in prayer while the women are preparing the body for burial. We should probably pay our respects." He glanced at the phone in my hand. "Who did you call?"

"Hope. Don't worry, she doesn't know what's really going on."

"You didn't call your pack?"

I shook my head.

"That's good," he said. "That would be like throwing kerosene on a fire, and this tribe's in no state of mind to be confronted by a pack they don't know. As for the locals, I don't know what the hell they would do. Look, I know how it seems, but Shikoba's not keeping you prisoner. He's protecting you. Your pack would only bring danger." Lakota regarded me for a moment. "Sometimes a wolf has to stand alone to find out what he's made of."

Tears glittered in my eyes. "I have to get home, Lakota. My dreams are crashing down around me."

He reached out and gripped my hand tight. "Your life is more important than your dreams."

A single tear rolled down my cheek. "My dreams *are* my life."

Lakota pinned me with those beautiful topaz-blue eyes. "Trust the fates, Melody. They put you here for a reason."

"To die?"

"I'm not going to let you die."

His words caused a flutter in my belly. They weren't just empty promises you said to make someone feel better. He meant them.

Turning away, I faced my reflection in the mirror. "I've almost died twice. Both times, you saved me. Maybe you shouldn't have. What if I'm not meant to be here and I'm living on borrowed time? What if I was supposed to die in the Breed war all those years ago when that wolf attacked me? Maybe you interfered with the fates, so they tried again years later."

There. I'd said it. The niggling thought in the back of my head that I'd carried with me for half my life.

I spun around. "Maybe I'm dreamwalking and none of this is real—it's just a figment of my imagination because I can't let go of life. What if I died and I'm refusing to let go? Maybe that's why my dreams are crumbling."

He rose before me like a tower and lowered his forehead until it touched mine. "You're not a spirit. Don't you think I would know if I had spooned a ghost?"

I chuckled softly and wiped my tears.

Lakota tenderly threaded my hair away from my face, his knuckles lightly brushing against my cheeks. "That's survivor's guilt talking. Other people died in the war, and you didn't, so you feel like you've got to make something of your life, or it's all for nothing. That's not how it works, Mel." He tipped his head to the side. "I've always seen you as a tough spirit, but now I'm getting to see a softer side. Remember when I said that my wolf has never found peace since that night I found you in the snowstorm?"

"Yeah."

"I lied."

Though I'd been looking at his mouth, I swung my gaze up to his eyes. "What do you mean?"

"I had that same feeling one other time. It was the moment I walked into the bar yesterday and saw you sitting there. That same feeling. Like..." He shook his head. "I don't know. I wish I knew the right words."

Lakota knew the right words, but he couldn't speak them aloud. He had the courage, but the situation with the tribe was too delicate. The moment he'd first laid eyes on her in that bar, his wolf practically vibrated beneath his skin, filling him with a sense of contentment he'd never thought possible. It was like coming home.

He'd always assumed that heroic act of rescuing a young girl was what had made his wolf respond, but he hadn't felt the same magnetic pull when he'd saved her from a bloodthirsty wolf years prior. Then again, she was just a child at the time. On that winter's night, Melody was on the cusp of becoming a woman, and his wolf had used his body to shield her from the deathly cold. In all his years working as a bounty hunter, he'd never been able to recreate that same rush. Not when he took down criminals, not even when he saved lives.

And he'd saved many lives.

Now that Melody had grown into a stunning young woman, he wasn't sure where he stood. She beguiled him with her familiarity and unfamiliarity all at once. He knew her—but he didn't. His wolf sensed her wolf for the first time, and they had an undeniable chemistry.

Or maybe it was the way her milky-green eyes looked at him with secrets behind those irises. He thought about those pouty lips and the way they'd latched on to his, making him burn for her. She fit perfectly against him, as if his body were made to protect her. He remembered the smell of her hair when he'd nuzzled close behind her while they slept together.

Slept.

Lakota had never imagined that simply holding a woman in bed could be so gratifying. How could sex possibly top hearing a woman's heart beating against his chest—feeling the rise and fall of her breath as she entrusted him with her life?

For years he'd seen her as unbreakable and determined. Never once had it occurred to him that the reason behind her ambition had to do with the guilt of simply surviving something. That knowledge made Lakota feel closer to understanding her.

Yet one thing bothered him. Melody still hadn't embraced her natural brown hair color. Lakota didn't care if she shaved her head or dyed it silver; the vibrant shades had become her signature look. No, it was the reasoning behind it. She'd once confided in him that she colored her hair because she felt unremarkable.

Melody had no clue just how remarkable she was—how infectious her creativity and love for life was to those around her. She possessed a warrior's heart and always wanted to be equal to men in every regard. She chased her dreams, even at the risk of failing, and held on to life with such ferocity that she shone brighter than any star in the sky. How could she possibly believe that her looks defined her worth as a woman?

It was puzzling how she and Hope had become such fast friends. Melody was the risk-taker, whereas Hope was more concerned about disappointing people. His sister had a gracious heart, and that goodness made him want to intervene in their business affairs. What kind of brother would he be if he didn't do everything within his power to make her happy? That gave him pause about the whole Shikoba situation. Somehow he needed to make it right.

But he also had a job to do.

Lakota opened the back door to Shikoba's property. Melody had opted to return to the kitchen and stay out of sight. Koi's wolf was lying on a bed of flowers, surrounded by women. Someone had cleaned the blood from his fur and stitched up the wounds.

One at a time, each of Koi's packmates approached his body, knelt, and honored him with private farewells. As they rose, they sliced a dagger across their hearts, and rivulets of blood trailed down their chests. Koi's mother sat close, and each packmate bestowed her with a gift, as was their custom. Some brought her food, while others gave trinkets or tokens. When a Shifter died, he remained in whatever form he was in at the time of death. It must have been hard for the family not to see his human face again, but they treated his wolf with the utmost respect.

Tak met him at the door, feathers in his hair and paint across his chest. "Come."

Lakota glanced at the old mother. "I don't have a gift."

Tak wrapped his arm around his shoulders and led him toward the body. "You brought her the most sacred gift of all—her son. My father doesn't deal with the Council, so had you not gone, we never would have gotten him back."

When Tak branched away, Lakota knelt in front of the grieving mother and bowed his head. He whispered a prayer in his native tongue and then rested his hand on the flowers beneath Koi.

Lakota's throat closed when the mother's hand covered his and moved it onto Koi's head. She said something in her language to the effect of "My son's spirit wolf is free now." He couldn't understand all of it, but when she finished, he stood up and searched for Shikoba.

Majestic trees that bordered the expansive grounds swayed, sending a kaleidoscope of fractured light onto the grass. A few trees had round slices of wood nailed to them that served as target practice for archers. Lakota glanced at the small cabin across from the house, near the tree line. Single ladies stayed there during their heat cycle to have privacy. Any good pack had something similar set up. Otherwise their hormonal impulses might cause them to make reckless decisions that could lead to pregnancy. A woman could only get pregnant while in heat; any time outside that was rare. Lakota had been around a woman in heat once or twice, and damn, it was a powerful thing. Their pheromones were an aphrodisiac, and unmated men—weak men—would say anything to seduce them.

He spotted Shikoba speaking to one of the elders. Not wanting to interrupt, Lakota nodded at him that he was ready to talk.

After Shikoba wrapped up his conversation, he gripped his cane and headed over. "Let's take this inside."

Melody would be fine in the kitchen, but he still didn't like leaving her alone, *especially* not after the way Kaota had come at her so aggressively. Just thinking about those marks on her arm made Lakota's wolf snarl.

When they reached Shikoba's private sitting room, they took their seats.

Shikoba propped his cane between his legs and gripped the wooden arms of the chair. "What did you find out, and what is the Council saying?"

Each territory had a local Council comprised of a small group of Shifters. They enforced the laws in the area and tried to keep order, but the tribe lived outside their laws.

"They called in a Vampire to scrub the memory of the animal control guy," Lakota said. "They were going to do an autopsy and give a report to police, so the Council made sure that didn't happen."

"And what will the police say when they get no report?"

"Shit gets lost all the time." Lakota moved his legs farther apart and turned his gaze toward a painting of a warrior on horseback. "The local packs are crying foul, saying the tribes are nothing but rapists and murderers and that the Council is sweeping it under the rug. They're accusing you of the deaths of the women, but that's been a quiet rumor for some time now."

Shikoba touched one of his thin braids. "Some things never change. We have lived here for many lifetimes, and outsiders have wanted our land for centuries. The soil is good, the stream plentiful with fish, and the woods abundant with animals to hunt. They have been waiting for this day. And do you know what casts a black cloud over all this?"

"What?"

"That they might be right about the killer." Shikoba drew in a deep breath. "I love my people, but even the most trusted man can blacken his spirit with envy, lust, or hate."

Lakota's thoughts briefly turned to his birth father. "If that's true, you can't shelter him to protect your people. You have to follow their laws and turn him in. I'm not saying you know who it is, but keep an open mind."

Shikoba jerked forward. "If I find out one of my men was responsible, I will kill him myself!" he thundered, slamming the bottom of his cane against the wood floor. "And if it was Koi"—he shook his head—"it would shame his poor mother more than you know. We were unable to tell whether the woman made those marks on him in self-defense or if he took his own life. Out of respect for his mother, we didn't want to shave his fur to inspect them closer."

"You have to get to the bottom of this," Lakota advised. "Let me go out to the crime scene."

"And what good will that do? The humans have trampled all over it."

"The rain and humidity will make it easy to pick up lingering scents. We need to scout the area for tracks and evidence. Maybe we can't prove who's guilty, but we should at least prove that Koi is innocent. I come from a long line of skilled trackers, and—"

"I'll send Tak with you. He's an alpha with a keen nose. Let him be the one to shift."

"I'll call the Council and make it happen. Since one of your packmates is dead, they have to honor your right to a fair investigation."

"All this publicity," Shikoba murmured. "And what of the white woman? Who will watch her while you're gone? My people are grieving."

Lakota gripped the arms of the chair. "She'll come with me. I'll keep an eye on her. She's not going to run off in the woods with her car still here."

In truth, he could have left her alone, but without knowing who was behind the murders, he didn't want to take the chance. The only way Lakota could keep her safe was to keep her close.

"We can't take the road out while those men are still there," Lakota remarked while rubbing his chin. "The bodies were found ten miles north, just beyond your territory near the Sanderson pack. Lend me one of your horses, and we'll go out the back way. I'll call the Council and make sure the crime scene is clear."

"And how do you know they won't set a trap? You can't trust the Council."

"I don't think they want a confrontation any more than we do."

What Lakota failed to mention was that he had a contact within the Council who knew his identity. With the higher authority being a higher level of law, the Council was sworn to secrecy when it came to investigative matters. They had no jurisdiction over bounty hunters hired by the higher authority.

"And you trust this woman not to run?" Shikoba pressed. "Not to scream for help or turn on you?"

Lakota leaned forward, propping his forearms on his knees. "Malevolence isn't exclusive to any one skin color, Breed, or gender. If you are judging her based on her skin, then you are no better than the rest of them."

"We are holding her against her will. She does not understand the hatred that has festered among some of the older packs, and since she's an outsider, they might want to punish her and use her as an example."

"Let me take the woman and give your family time to

grieve alone. You have my word that I won't let anything happen to her. We'll be back before the ceremony tonight. She won't run. I can promise you that."

"I have no reason to trust her," Shikoba said matter-of-factly. "But I trust your wolf. You brought my nephew home and gave peace to his family. Go find out what you can and bring me this information. I only hope we have not angered the spirits in some way."

Lakota hoped the same, or else it could all end in bloodshed.

CHAPTER 11

"WHOSE IDEA WAS IT TO bring me along on this fun-filled horseback adventure?" I held on tight to Lakota, my rear end as sore as everything.

We climbed a hill, and Lakota hugged his calves against the horse, holding the reins and coaxing him on.

When he ignored me, I kept talking. "Shouldn't I be the one in the front?"

"Maybe she would rather hold on to a man and not a boy," Tak suggested with a peal of laughter. "It's not too late to ride with me, little flower." He raced ahead of us. When his white horse crested the hill, she whinnied and pawed at the ground.

My thighs hadn't been this sore since the last time I played laser tag with my brothers. It had been at least two hours since we'd left, though it felt more like ten. The lack of wind wasn't helping, nor was the occasional mosquito. *What I wouldn't give to be back home.*

Poor Hope was probably breaking her back setting up the store while I was busy riding to a crime scene on horseback, my arms wrapped around her brother's midsection. *What has my life become?*

We finally ascended the hill and continued our journey on level ground.

I tugged Lakota's hair. "How many people live in the tribe?"

Lakota peered over his shoulder. "Hundreds. They're spread apart in different territories. Same tribe."

I wiped the sweat from my brow.

"There's no escape," Tak added, giving me a stern look. "No running." He galloped ahead of us, his long braid flapping against his bare back.

"So... what happens with all the alphas?"

"They form small groups—the same as packs. Some head over to other territories in the region to either check out their women or see if there's room. Since they don't follow the Council's rules, they look to their elders. It's a pretty sophisticated beehive."

"Huh." I pinched my tank top in front and fanned my chest as I pulled the fabric out. "Did Koi normally come out this far to fish and hunt? Seems a little out of the way."

Lakota loosened his grip on his Appaloosa's reins. "He died in wolf form, so it seems logical that his wolf ran out this far."

"But the murder happened *off* tribal land. If the tribe marks their territory lines like we do, his wolf shouldn't have wandered past them. Did anyone find his clothes?"

He turned his head, showing me his handsome profile. "You ask smart questions."

"Need a partner if this boutique idea doesn't pan out?"

Tak galloped toward us, and his horse reared. "We're here. I don't see any humans, but keep your eyes alert."

I admired the quiver slung over his left shoulder, a wooden bow secured to it. I missed my bow, and the thought of it lying in pieces in the back of the Jeep made me sick to my stomach. We reached a small clearing where a hiking trail curved around a large rock.

Tak slid off his horse and tied the reins to a tree. "How much time do we have?"

Lakota held out his arm for me to take and dismount. I

clutched his hand and grimaced when my feet touched the ground.

"We have until dusk. The Council doesn't think anyone will try to come out here after dark, but don't count on it." Lakota leaned forward and swung his leg over the back of the horse before sliding off. "Some of the tracks belong to cops, so it's going to be messy."

Tak handed his weapons to Lakota. When I realized he was going to shift, I clutched Lakota's arm and pressed myself close.

Tak smiled. "Don't worry, little flower. I'm an alpha."

That should have reassured me since it meant he could govern his wolf's actions when in animal form, but it didn't. Tak was a stranger to me, and while alphas were stereotypically protective of women, there was always an element of danger in the company of wolves.

In a fluid movement, Tak shifted into a black-and-grey wolf. Half of his face was black and the other half grey, mirroring his tattooed markings. He trotted around the area in search of a scent.

"Where did it happen?" I asked, walking in Lakota's footsteps.

He scanned the ground, his pace sedate. Lakota's stepfather was a talented tracker, and combined with the fact that his adoptive father was a Chitah, he had knowledge under his belt that suited him for a job like this. He crouched and plucked a blade of grass, then turned it in his hand. "Blood spatter."

Tak's wolf circled around a grassy area by the dirt path.

"Did you find something, Tak?" Lakota headed toward him and knelt down on one knee. "Careful where your wolf walks. I haven't compared all the tracks yet."

I stepped onto the dirt path and out of the way, watching them examine a flattened patch of grass.

"This is where she died," Lakota said, wiping his mouth with one hand.

Since I hadn't heard any details about the murder, I asked, "How did it happen? Are they saying the wolf attacked her?"

"They're saying anything they want to imagine. Some are saying his wounds were self-defense, while others suggest a murder-suicide. There's a lot of blood pooled here... and here. Looks like she had two major wounds." Lakota's eyes skated to the right, and he bent down with his face to the ground. He picked up a cigarette butt and smelled it. "It's fresh."

"What kind?"

He twisted his mouth. "Can't tell, but it's got a weird filter."

"We're on a hiking trail," I pointed out. "The woods are probably littered with them."

Lakota swung his gaze up at me. "Yesterday's rain would have ruined the paper. Someone put this out either last night or this morning. It might have been a cop, but the killer could have also returned to the scene. Maybe he left something behind. Dammit, I wish we'd found the body before them. There are too many footprints."

I wiped my chin and longed for a cool breeze. My jeans were too hot for outdoor recreation. Tak's wolf sniffed the entire perimeter around the tree line while Lakota scanned the open ground for clues. I wondered if it was possible that the police had missed something. This wasn't exactly the big city, and I would wager that their police force consisted of a sheriff and two deputies.

The sight of the bloody stains in the grass gave me chills, and whenever a leaf rustled in the woods because of a squirrel scampering up a tree, I jumped.

"Lakota?"

Wielding a stick, he rose to his feet and swaggered toward me. "Yeah?"

"If the outside Shifters think Koi was the killer, how do they explain him doing it right next to a hiking trail? Wouldn't he have wanted to commit the murder somewhere more private? Anyone could have walked up on them."

Lakota glowered as he stared at the path and then back at the patch of grass. "I think we have enough evidence that Koi wasn't the killer. The pack looked him over and said he died from deep wounds to the jugular. Why would she shift and engage in a struggle only to shift back and put on her clothes? I bet Koi knew her and they were meeting here. Like you said, he wouldn't have run off the territory in wolf form. I bet his attacker stole his clothes."

"Why would he do that?"

He shrugged. "All the cops found was a dead girl and a wolf. Leaving clothes behind would open up a manhunt, and maybe he didn't want the local police to initiate a search."

Tak shifted to human form and strode toward us, completely naked and his long hair unbound. "There's blood everywhere, but it's not the girl's. She didn't run or fight. It looks like her death was quick. But someone else was here. I can't find any tracks, but I found a few drops of blood that weren't Koi's."

"You're sure?" Lakota asked.

Tak lifted his chin. "Koi died protecting that girl. His wolf had blood in his mouth, and I guarantee it wasn't hers."

Lakota handed the cigarette to Tak and let him look at it. "At least we can confirm his innocence with Shikoba. The packs won't believe it, but Koi's mother will have peace of mind. Did you recognize any scents?"

Tak rubbed his nose. "Too many ingredients in the stew. It all smells the same. I tasted Koi's blood and the victim's, but there's another flavor on my tongue I picked up near the spatter by the trees."

"You can't pick up the scent?"

Tak narrowed his eyes. "If I taste his blood again, I'll know. But his scent is long gone."

Lakota glanced up at the sky. "We should go before a nosy reporter decides to send a chopper out here."

Tak snorted. "They don't have the budget for gas. They'll recycle the chopper footage since the station is too far and there are other stories in the city to report. Nobody cares what happens out here in the wild." Tak turned to gather his clothes. "My father will be pleased. He respected Koi, even though he sometimes hung his shoes on the clothesline."

I froze when savage growls erupted from the bush to my left. My eyes widened as four wolves emerged from a thicket of trees. Based on Tak and Lakota's reactions, they didn't belong to the tribe.

Lakota glanced at the horses, but they were at least thirty feet away. "You need to get out of here," he ordered me. "We're off the territory."

In a fluid movement, Tak shifted to wolf form and stalked toward them, his gait heavy because of his size and power. He was trying to get them to submit—something less dominant wolves sometimes did around an alpha. Of the four wolves, not one of them appeared to be the leader. Perhaps the alpha was hiding.

"We're not trespassing on private property, are we?" I asked.

"This isn't Shifter land. They don't have a right to be here any more than we do. Stay behind me." Lakota curved his arm around my body and herded me out of their sight.

My mind scrambled. *Oh my God, am I going to have to shift?* I swallowed hard, mentally counting the steps to the horses and wondering how fast I could mount. I spotted Tak's quiver and bow leaning against a tree. More terrifying than death was not knowing how vicious those wolves were. They might shift to human form and force me to do things that... I gripped Lakota's shirt, my heart pounding.

Lakota slowly turned his head and locked eyes with me. "Look submissive."

I felt a flush of insult at those words.

Submissive?

Before I could argue, I blinked and found myself holding his T-shirt. Lakota had shifted into a gorgeous silver wolf, every bit as large as Tak's. He had the most exquisite coat—

pale silver that was a rarity among Shifters because of the uniformity of coloring. His only marking was the black liner around his blue eyes.

He communicated to me with those eyes. *Stay close but not too close.*

The four wolves advanced, and Tak gave a warning growl. Unless defending territory or a packmate, most wolves avoided deadly conflict. At the moment, I wasn't sure what we were defending except for our lives.

Lakota backed up against me, using his body as a shield as he bared his teeth. As instructed, I kept my eyes submissively low and never made eye contact. Their growls and snarls sent a shiver up my spine, reminding me that they had us outnumbered. I could imagine those teeth snapping at me, and I knew exactly how they would feel. The scars on my right foot served as a reminder that no one was safe from bad men—not children, not women, not innocents. That attack had been a blessing in disguise, making me less naive.

Tension mounted. The birds fluttering in the nearby trees fell silent, as if sensing an impending battle.

Without warning, a wolf lunged at Tak, viciously snapping at his neck. Lakota assailed the largest wolf and locked his jaw around its throat. When the remaining two wolves swung their gazes toward Lakota and Tak, I fled.

My feet barely touched the ground. I reached the horses in no time flat and snatched the quiver. My hands trembled as I held the bow and pulled out an arrow.

"Stay calm, stay calm," I whispered, nocking my arrow and then pulling back the bowstring. I was panting hard and trying to steady my breath.

Tak's horse whinnied as the wolves savagely thrashed one another about.

"*Move,*" I hissed.

They were like a cyclone of energy, circling and jumping so quickly that I couldn't get a clear shot. Lakota's wolf ruthlessly drew blood from a brown wolf caught between his massive jaws. When a third wolf whirled around and bit Lakota on his haunch, my shot was clear and my aim was true.

The arrow sliced through the air and struck the rogue in the side. The red wolf yelped and toppled over, immediately shifting to human form. He still had the arrow buried in his chest, and everyone knew that shifting with an object inside you could cause permanent damage. That was why many Natives still used archaic weapons. Heck, even my grandmother used a bow.

Tak rose up on his hind legs in an impressive display. He then collided with one of the wolves in a violent tornado. I lined up another arrow.

Lakota's rival wriggled free and circled around him faster than a heartbeat. I held my breath and pulled the bowstring taut. Just as I let go, my target caught sight of me and turned. The arrow grazed his leg, which galvanized him into action. The whites of his eyes gleamed as he barreled after me, his fangs wet with blood.

When Lakota realized what was happening, he gave chase. There wasn't time to pull out another arrow.

I had no alternative.

I shifted.

Lakota's muscles burned like fire as he tore after the wolf. He had the ability to stay awake for several minutes into his shift before blacking out, so he needed to utilize every second. When Melody's eyes widened with fear, he dug his nails into the dirt, gathering speed. *Catch him. Catch him.*

His heart nearly stopped when Melody shifted and fled. He barely had time to process it since his eyes were locked on the wolf. He slammed into him with brute force, and they rolled across a bed of leaves. When the wolf reared around and sank his fangs into Lakota's shoulder, a second shot of adrenaline kicked in and gave him the energy needed to take on the large animal. Lakota used his hind legs to throw the wolf off-balance and end the fight as quickly as he could. Tak was battling two wolves, and Lakota wasn't sure about the third, who'd gone down after Melody struck him with an arrow.

When the wolf lost his balance and fell onto his side, Lakota lunged for the exposed jugular. Blood filled his mouth as he thrashed violently until the wolf finally went still. Without a second to spare, he turned around and charged back into the fray.

Tak had one of the wolves pinned, but a second wolf had bitten his back and looked like he was attempting to tug hard enough to pull the hide off. Lakota crashed into him, and they struck a tree. He bulldozed the animal with his merciless gaze, and when he saw a flicker of fear, he knew the battle was over. With lightning speed, the wolf escaped in the opposite direction.

Lakota felt his awareness dimming, so he shifted to human form and then back to his wolf, the wounds on his shoulder and leg healing. He waited to see if Tak needed help, but the situation seemed under control. Lakota shifted back and stalked toward the wolf Melody had taken down. He had half a mind to shove that arrow right back where it belonged and finish him off, but the idiot had done enough damage by shifting while it was still in him—enough that it had knocked him unconscious from either pain or blood loss.

Tak morphed into human form when the wolf beneath him fell still.

"Do you know them?" Lakota asked, out of breath.

"Local rogues." Tak nudged the dead wolf with his foot. "They don't belong to a pack."

Lakota wiped the blood from his face. "What the hell are they doing out here?"

Tak's expression darkened like a thundercloud. "Looking for trouble, and they found it."

"We need to get out of here. Now that the cops are done

with their crime scene, it won't take long before people in town get curious and want to check this place out, and here we are, bathed in blood."

Tak swiped his arrow off the ground and cursed. "Those wolves are going to lie to the Council. That *chickenshit* who ran off was an alpha."

Lakota raised his eyebrows in surprise. Usually he could sense an alpha, so it must have been a weak one.

"That means he saw us with the girl," Tak continued, blood trickling down his back. "Rumors are going to fly. Two Natives hanging around a crime scene with another white girl—they're going to call it sacrificial or some bullshit."

Yanking up his pants, Lakota said, "The girl took off. We need to find her before she winds up on someone's territory."

While they were heading back to the horses, Tak reached over his shoulder to an unhealed wound that was leaking a lot of blood. "Maybe we should just let her go."

"Yeah, nothing suspicious about that. Girl goes missing, last seen with us, and they find her Jeep on your land."

After Tak shifted once and back again, he put on his pants and collected his weapons off the ground. His mare was rattled, so he took the reins and stroked her neck, his voice soothing and firm. "Easy, girl. I know you love me."

But Lakota's Appaloosa wasn't showing him any love. It backed away when he neared it.

Tak slung his quiver over his shoulder and mounted. "Approach her like you would a woman in bed: slow and easy."

Lakota flashed him a peevish glance before he untied the reins and mounted. "Maybe my women like to be tackled."

"I didn't know you liked football players."

They clucked their tongues and headed into the woods.

Once Tak's horse learned the direction they were heading, Tak let go of the reins and began plaiting his hair. "Women like to see your intent. You've got to treat her gently—ease up on her and make her feel safe. She has to trust you before you decide to lift that skirt and make her feel like a woman."

Lakota's horse picked up speed. "Maybe you frighten women too easily, and that's why you have to crawl on them like a snail."

Tak finished tying off his hair and shrugged off the comment. "I can't deny that. Women don't like to look at my face."

"I didn't think it was your face they were busy looking at."

Two warriors, fresh from a kill, laughed like schoolboys.

They veered right, the horses huffing as they climbed a steep embankment. Once they reached the top, Lakota dismounted. Tak's horse pranced in a circle, still full of energy.

They'd been following Melody's tracks, but those tracks had begun turning in circles, indicating that her wolf had stopped to rest. She would be tired, and the heat was oppressive without any wind for relief. Lakota led his horse toward the sound of splashing water.

"There's a swimming hole up ahead," Tak said. "I bet she stopped for a drink."

Lakota stalked through the thinning brush. He could smell the water and hear it trickling. As he ducked beneath a vine, he spotted a wolf on the edge of a flat rock just ahead. He slowed his pace when he saw the cliff, his hands up. "Easy, girl." From his position, he couldn't tell how steep the drop was. Lakota kept a watchful eye on her hind legs, which were precariously close to the edge.

Lakota was silenced by her beauty. Melody reminded him of a patchwork quilt with her unique coloring. She looked like a white wolf someone had painted orange and brown markings on. The contrast was mesmerizing. Usually the multicolored wolves had more mottled coats, but the white on hers stood out like freshly fallen snow.

Her green eyes were fierce, but she kept her head submissively low. A growl rumbled in her chest when she noticed Tak approaching.

"I got this," Tak said with cool confidence. He stalked past

Lakota and stopped between them. "The women may run, but their wolves always know a good alpha when they see one."

Melody's lips peeled back, and she licked her fangs.

"Careful, Tak. She's not from around here," Lakota reminded him.

Tak turned around, a smug grin on his face. "Let me take care of this. I'm not going to hurt her."

Lakota folded his arms. "No, but she might hurt you."

As if insulted, Tak lifted his chin. "I'm like the Pied Piper. Watch me work my magic."

Melody's wolf backed up a step, a chunk of rock breaking off and falling below. Lakota drew in a sharp breath.

"I'm not going to hurt you," Tak said smoothly, advancing toward her. His alpha power rippled through the air. "Calm down and submit like a good girl." Her wolf wouldn't understand his words, but she would feel the meaning behind them.

Tak froze when Melody suddenly streaked toward him. She leapt into the air like an experienced warrior and threw him onto his back. Before he could push her off, she charged at Lakota and knocked the wind out of him. He flew backward and hit the ground, her wolf straddling him.

She lunged viciously at his face, but instead of attacking, she licked it clean.

Tak stood and brushed the leaves from his pants. Not that Lakota could see much of what Tak was doing. Melody's wolf was wiggling, flapping her tail, whining, and licking him all over his mouth and face. He wasn't certain whether she wanted to befriend him or gobble him up like an ice cream cone.

Tak appeared in his line of vision and bent over, his hands on his knees. "She acts like she's known you all her life."

Lakota shoved her off when he heard a current of suspicion in Tak's voice. Without warning, Melody ran at breakneck speed toward the cliff and leapt off the edge. Both men chased after her and skidded to a stop when they reached the rock.

Twenty feet below was a swimming hole, and her wolf was paddling in the water like a duck.

Tak stripped out of his pants and shoes and tossed them over the edge to where the bank was. "Someone has the right idea. Why don't you bring the horses down for a drink?" He dove off the edge, hugging his knees, and created a loud splash when he hit the water like a cannonball. Seconds later, Tak's head appeared above the surface, and he whooped with delight.

Irritated, Lakota grabbed the horses and headed left until he found an easy path that led down to the riverbank.

Why am I so damn mad? At first he thought it had to do with Melody's wolf almost blowing his cover. Tak could have caught on and realized something was up. But in truth, Lakota wanted to jump in the water and play with her wolf. He wanted to be as easy with her as Tak was. It was the first time he'd met her wolf, and that was an honor among Shifter family and friends. He wondered how differently their meeting would have gone had they been alone—how he would have cradled her wolf in his arms and shown his affection. Now her first memory of Lakota was going to be him shoving her away. Her wolf didn't know anything about bounty hunting and undercover operations. She didn't deserve to be punished with his ambivalence.

And that first impression might be a lasting one.

When the horses caught sight of water, they trotted ahead of him. Their hooves splashed in the shallow end as they lowered their heads to drink. Lakota left them and headed up the bank to the right, noticing a small waterfall within the retreat. Melody's wolf had claimed a flat rock beside it. Her head tilted to the side at the naked man floating on his back.

"Get in here!" Tak yelled. "Life doesn't get better than this."

No sense in arguing. The heat was sweltering, and the cool water sang to Lakota like a siren's song. He stripped out of his clothes and dove in. The water shocked him for all of three seconds, then it was just cold, clean, and refreshing.

He swam to the middle, the dried blood washing off his skin. "Koi's in the clear, but do you think one of your packmates might have killed that girl?"

Tak closed his eyes when a shower of sunlight trickled through the branches overhead and caught him in a net of light. "I don't think it was one of ours," he said, his legs sinking as he righted himself. "Only white men kill for sport, and all those other victims were a sporting event."

"Or a lesson. It could go either way."

Tak swam toward the shore and got out. "Do you *want* to implicate my people?"

"No, but you can't point fingers until you've eliminated all motive. If it's one of the outsiders, they'll eventually be caught and punished. But if it *is* someone in your tribe, don't go down with them for the sake of protecting one of your own. There's a lot of animosity in this town. I see it in everyone's eyes, even yours."

After putting on his pants, Tak sat on the bank, his knees drawn up and his arms draped over them. "Who are the ones that sit in the back of the bar? Who has to park behind the building in the mud? Who has to be careful about shifting off the property, or else they could be killed? We are prisoners in our own community. You don't see that damn goat getting served on toast whenever he shifts in the bar, but what would happen if one of *us* shifted in there?"

Lakota dipped his head back and drenched his hair. "Maybe it's time for you to put aside your differences and learn to get along. Start making changes. The whole world isn't like Running Horse, you know."

Tak narrowed his eyes. "Violence is the only real thing that makes changes. Just look at history. Half the Shifters around here are rogues looking for a good piece of land away from humans—land that belongs to us. They don't want to make friends with my kind. They're waiting for an opportunity to drive us off our territory."

Treading water, Lakota gave the matter some thought. He could see motive on both sides. The tribes resented the locals and might have lashed out in anger, or perhaps their logic was to eliminate women so the outside Shifters couldn't breed anymore. The packs and rogues obviously wanted the land and were digging their heels in. It was prime real estate—more miles of property than one could dream of owning. Or perhaps the killer was neither. Maybe it was just a sadistic murderer or someone who wanted to start a war between Breed and humans by planting Shifter bodies within human reach.

Melody's wolf stood up, pacing restlessly the way Shifters did when their human spirit was ready to take over. After lapping up a few mouthfuls of water, she crouched down and then jumped off the rock, shifting in midair.

CHAPTER 12

T HE SECOND I HIT THE water, I flailed my arms in panic. *Where am I? Is someone still chasing me?* The thoughts ricocheted in my mind as I choked on water.

The last thing I remembered was shifting when a wolf came after me. My wolf and I shared one purpose, one thought—*survive.* As consciousness had dissipated and my human spirit fell asleep, I knew my wolf would protect us and run like the wind.

Now I was choking and gasping for air, disoriented and unable to feel the ground beneath my feet. A loud splash sounded ahead, and Lakota was swimming in my direction.

He scooped his arm around my waist and whispered, "Are you okay?"

I held on to his neck. Water had shot up my nose, and I was coughing and gasping in a mad struggle to breathe. Normally I was a good swimmer, but the coughing made it difficult to speak, let alone swim.

"Hang on," he said. "I've got you."

With one arm, he swam toward the shore. As I held on, I suddenly realized how naked I was against him. Not only that, but how naked *he* was.

I let go and tried to wriggle out of his grasp, but he had an iron grip around my waist. Meanwhile, my breasts were precariously close to revealing themselves to his bestie, who was sitting on the shore, watching with avid interest.

When I felt the rocks beneath my feet, I used my heels to dig in and wrench away.

Lakota turned to face me. "What are you doing?"

My gaze darted between them. Nudity wasn't normally a big deal, but maybe it was a little different because I liked Lakota. Maybe I wasn't ready for him to see my body in its entirety, especially with an audience.

I didn't know his friend well enough, and we were in the middle of the wilderness in unfamiliar territory.

"Where are the wolves?" I asked.

When Lakota stood, the waterline was just below his navel. "Dead and gone."

Tak smirked. "Some dead, some gone. You're a good shot with a bow."

I wiped my face. "Not good enough. I missed the second one."

Lakota gave me a wolfish smile. "You might want to cover your eyes."

"Only if you promise to do the same."

He swiped his finger across his heart and stalked away. Water splashed from the movement of his powerful legs, and even though I had my hands shielding my eyes, I couldn't resist sneaking a peek between two fingers.

Oh. My. God. I'd never seen anything as glorious as Lakota's backside. He had a strong physique with broad shoulders and taut muscles, but his ass was sculpted to perfection. He glistened, and his wet hair looked like spun silk the way it flattened between his shoulder blades. Every part of him was perfectly proportioned, and it made me want to dunk my head under the water and hide. A man didn't go around looking like that without realizing he was an Adonis.

I'll die if he sees me naked! I'd never been as self-conscious about my body as the second he turned and looked at me.

"Your turn," he said. "We have to get moving before dark."

Keeping my hands over my eyes while he put on his pants, I asked, "Are you done?"

Tak chuckled and stood up. "This is better than TV."

I dropped my hands in the water and searched the area. "Where are my pants?"

They exchanged looks, and sheer horror swept over me.

"Tell me you didn't leave my clothes behind."

Lakota squeezed the water from the ends of his hair. "No worries. I saw a few big leaves back there. Maybe you can sew a dress."

My jaw set. "You're not funny."

A robust laugh rolled out of Tak, and he turned away. "That's up for debate."

"Then shift," Lakota suggested.

I tilted my head to the side. "My wolf isn't going to follow you."

Tak kept laughing. "That's also up for debate."

This was awful. Terrible! I wasn't even sure how close we were to the house, and the idea of riding on horseback naked while holding on to Lakota was... kind of sexy. But not so much with Tak around.

"Come out of there," Lakota ordered. "You're being childish."

I almost fired a comeback but snapped my mouth shut when I remembered no one was supposed to know that we were old acquaintances. "Modesty and childishness might appear the same to you, but someday I'd like to give my body to my mate as a gift without the whole world having seen it first."

Tak arched his eyebrows and gave me a respectful nod. "I'd give you my pants, but then *my* modesty would be compromised." He clapped his hand on Lakota's shoulder. "I'll just leave you two alone to figure this out while I round up the horses."

When Tak was out of earshot, I admonished Lakota with

one glance. "I see *you* took the time to get dressed, but you left my clothes behind? Those were my favorite pants."

He pinched his chin. "Let's just worry about one thing at a time." After a stretched-out minute, he stripped off his T-shirt and offered it to me.

I splashed water at him. "That's not going to cover up the important bits."

He snorted, amusement dancing in his eyes. "No one will see anything on horseback."

"Maybe I'm not enthusiastic about spreading my legs open on the back of a horse for the next five miles. That's a rash I don't want to deal with. Give me your pants."

He tossed the shirt on a rock. "Shall I tell you the reason why men shouldn't ride naked on horseback?"

"Then walk."

"Naked. In my shoes," he said, conveying the disrespectful scene we would give the tribe, who were in the middle of mourning one of their fallen.

It was an awful predicament.

Lakota glanced up at where Tak had gone. "We need to go, Mel. Get out of the water. Those wolves might have gone for backup."

"Does this stream run by the house?"

"Are you going to swim the whole way? I've got a better reason to get moving. There's a snake behind you."

Does he really think stooping to such immature tactics will frighten me? "There's no snake in here. Maybe I can fall back and let you two walk at a distance. One of you can ride ahead and—"

"Dammit, Mel. There's a snake!"

My eyes widened in horror when, in my periphery, a long reptilian creature slithered across the water in my direction. After that, my mind went blank.

A scream poured out of my mouth, and I charged out of the water with flailing arms and five pints of adrenaline shooting through my veins. I couldn't think straight or even feel my feet touching the ground. All I knew was that a giant anaconda was chasing me.

When I emerged naked from the water, Lakota stumbled backward with a startled expression and slammed his eyes shut before turning away.

I didn't just run to Lakota—I flew. Crawled right onto his back like a monkey climbing a tree, wrapping my arms tightly around his head.

"I can't see!" he bellowed.

"Where is it? Where is it?" I shouted. "Get it away from me!"

"It's not going to hurt you. It's not even a foot long."

Tak cleared his throat from somewhere above. "You two kids hurry up down there." His laughter echoed in the swimming hole, then faded as he walked away.

Lakota finally shook me off his back. "Look, it's harmless."

I shuddered when I saw the snake swimming away. "I *hate* snakes."

Since I'd grown up in the woods, wild animals were a part of life. But venomous snakes were particularly deadly to Shifters since shifting wouldn't eliminate the venom.

Lakota turned away from me, and despite everything that had just transpired, I felt a flicker of desire as rivulets of water dripped down his back. We were alone, wet, and mostly naked. A flutter of tingles surfaced in places that made me feel exposed and vulnerable.

"I'll shift," he finally said. "You can wear my clothes and ride back. My wolf will stay close, and Tak will keep him in line if anything unexpected happens. How's that for a plan? Acceptable?"

Walking naked to a funeral wasn't, so at this point, I was willing to take whatever options I could. "Promise not to wander far?"

His head turned but not enough that I could tell if he could see me. "Why?"

"I don't know Tak," I whispered. "And neither do you. Not really."

"I'll stay close." He swiftly shifted into his handsome wolf and licked my hand before racing off.

After putting on Lakota's T-shirt, I stepped into his jeans, which swallowed me. "I need to gain some weight," I muttered, laughing at the situation.

When I walked upstream and climbed the hill, I caught sight of Tak sitting on his horse, his hands gripping a branch overhead. I had half a mind to startle the mare and leave him dangling from the tree. But we had no time for mischievous behavior.

"Your friend shifted. He said he'll stay close," I called out.

Tak twisted around and looked me over. "So I see."

I approached the Appaloosa and hesitated. The horse didn't have a saddle to help me mount.

"Need a little help?" he offered.

Even though I did, the condescending tone of his voice was enough to make me dig in my heels. I circled around to the left side, and when I reached for her mane, my pants fell to my ankles.

Able to see my head and lower legs from the other side of the horse, Tak chuckled. This was going to be harder than I thought. I discreetly bent over and lifted the pants.

"Let me help you before the sun goes to bed." Tak hopped off his horse and moseyed around to my side. He lovingly stroked the mare's neck before locking his fingers and bending over. "Step up."

I gripped the waistband of my jeans on the right side to keep them secure. The moment I put my left foot between his cupped fingers, he launched me onto the back of the horse. Before I could situate myself, Tak slapped the mare on the rear, and she took off like a bolt of lightning.

As I bounced on the horse, struggling to hold on, my T-shirt flapped up and down and my pants slid so low that I could feel the wind on my ass.

So much for modesty.

Tak's boisterous laugh eventually faded once I rode out of earshot.

We traversed the woods for an hour before my thighs began to stiffen and ache. Lakota's wolf remained out of sight most of the time, but every so often, I would catch him peering at me through the trees. It comforted me unexpectedly, even though I wasn't in imminent danger. Just the idea of him looking out for me warmed my heart and made me curious about the man Lakota had become.

Yet the stronger my feelings for him grew, the more I wanted to distance myself. *A relationship with my best friend's brother?* Hope wouldn't like it, and neither would his family, especially his Shifter stepfather, who was all about heritage and passing along traditions.

Am I really sitting here contemplating a relationship? Perhaps it was more like finding reasons *not* to be in a relationship. Lakota was a bounty hunter and traveled a lot. Strike one. I had a business to run and no time for dealing with a mate who might be threatened by my ambition. Strike two. What if he never found a spot as a second-in-command and I was the one bringing home the bacon? Other men might give him a hard time about who wore the pants in the family. Would he eventually want me to stay home and make babies?

Am I really sitting here contemplating babies with Lakota?

The man had never had sex before, and he sure as heck wasn't going to mate the first woman he bedded. Life didn't work that way.

"You've been quiet the past mile," Tak said. "Something on your mind?"

Sex with Lakota? I wiped my forehead. "No. Just enjoying the scenery."

When Tak clucked his tongue, his horse trotted up beside

mine, matching its pace. "You know, it's none of my business, but you two seem very comfortable with each other." He straightened his back and looked skyward. "Sometimes a man is more afraid to make the first move when it's a woman he admires. She intimidates him. He's afraid she'll reject him, so it's better if he rejects her first."

"Sometimes the guy just doesn't like the girl."

He chuckled softly. "I know the look a man carries when his wolf has found a mate."

I snorted. "That's jumping the gun a little. We just met."

Tak shrugged. "It hardly matters if you've known someone a lifetime or a minute. Our wolves always know who they belong to." He leaned forward and petted his horse's neck. "So, little wildflower, does your wolf sing for Sky Hunter?"

I pressed my heels to get my horse to trot ahead of him. Tak came across as the tough guy who liked to get under people's skin for a laugh, and some of those jokes were hitting a nerve.

When we reached the house, only the women were outside.

"Where is everyone?" I asked.

Tak slowed his horse. "The men are preparing for the ceremony. In our tribe, when a man dies, the men paint their faces black so the spirit won't see them and hold on to this world. We hang out inside until dark and drink. The women stay with the body, sing to him, and prepare his soul to leave."

"And when a woman dies?"

He whispered something in his language and glared. "Don't say such things."

We reached the clearing at the far end of the backyard and dismounted.

Tak gathered the reins of both horses. "You'll stay in there," he said, pointing at the small cabin.

"And you?"

"We journey to the burial ground and stay overnight, singing prayers and sending our brother to his next journey. A stranger would confuse him. All of us go, even the little ones, so you'll be by yourself."

"Is there anything I can do?"

He cocked his head to the side, looking at me with surprise. "You're a compassionate wolf, but this is family. Stay inside the cabin tonight. His spirit will come back to remember his home and land before moving on, and it would be a bad omen if he saw you."

"Is it okay if I get my purse out of the kitchen?"

He nodded and led the horses away.

Keeping my eyes respectfully low, I passed by the women. Some were sitting around the fire, and others were busy making beaded necklaces. A white blanket covered the wolf's body, tucked around the edges to protect it. When I entered the house, it was eerily quiet. I hustled to the kitchen to retrieve my purse and spotted a bowl of fruit on the counter, which made my stomach growl. Lakota had given me a stern warning about taking food that wasn't offered, though he could have spared me the lecture since I wasn't brought up by jackals.

I dug around in my purse for my phone, but the battery had died. My phone charger was still in the Jeep, and I had a feeling that the small cabin out back wouldn't have any outlets. No matter. Checking messages could wait.

When I put the phone back, my fingers curled around the chain to my turquoise turtle pendant. I studied the intricate silver filigree framing every stone. As I headed back outside, gifts were sitting on top of a folded quilt. I left the pendant necklace on the blanket, then hurried to the cabin by the tree line. I didn't think Hope would mind, and it seemed like the appropriate thing to do.

Once inside the cabin, I closed the door and took a gander at my surroundings. I'd half expected it to be a dusty old shed full of spiders, but I was pleasantly surprised. Granted, it was small, no bigger than fifteen feet long and twelve feet wide. But it had all the essentials. The fireplace was made of stone, and a painting of a woman and child standing in a meadow hung over the mantle. Just to the right of the hearth was a tiny bathroom with a standing shower. A person could comfortably live here—eat at the table to the right, sit in the rocking chair by the door and have a beer, and retire at night in the small bed against the left wall. It had a brown-and-turquoise blanket that was clearly handmade. The cabin didn't have a kitchenette or even a closet, but it was cozy, welcoming, and beautifully decorated.

I stepped on the rug. *Wow.* Not a speck of dirt anywhere— not even in the fireplace, which probably hadn't been used since last winter. It wasn't as upscale as the heat house my former pack had built, but the cozy and rustic atmosphere made it feel like a retreat.

I set my purse on the table and looked down at the chopped wood piled by the fireplace. Since the cabin didn't have electricity, I gathered up candles and put them in the hearth. *Maybe later on, I can sit in the rocking chair and…*

Wait a second. What am I thinking? I need to get back home. This isn't a vacation, and what if my stay lasts for weeks? I gripped the rocker and stared vacantly at the fireplace. With everyone gone tonight, I would have a chance to escape. But I wasn't sure if that was the smart thing to do. I wasn't the enemy in the eyes of the Shifters outside their property, so surely they would let me pass. Still, I had a seed of doubt. Aside from that, I didn't want to be the catalyst for war because a few local yokels got the wrong idea. Maybe I didn't understand the Iwa tribe's perspective, but most of them seemed like good people who loved one another. Clearly they had a few hotheads, but Shikoba hadn't exactly shackled me to the cabin against my will.

The room felt like a sauna, so I turned the latch and opened the casement windows that overlooked the backyard. A cool breeze fluttered in and aired out the room. After stripping out of Lakota's clothes, I took a long shower. It had barely any water pressure, but at least I didn't smell like a creek anymore. I dried off, wrapped the towel around me, and tucked it in at the top. Just as I entered the main room, a knock sounded at the door.

I rushed out to greet Lakota. "It's about time. I thought—"

My words were cut off by the jarring sight of Shikoba in black face paint. What looked like bright-red tears were trailing down his face from each eye, and he was wearing an elaborate headdress of white feathers with black tips.

I stepped back to let him in.

He shook his head. "It's almost dusk, so we must go."

I nodded.

Shikoba reached around and revealed a large basket. "There's bread and dried meat."

I accepted the basket with reluctance. They had enough to worry about and shouldn't have gone to the trouble. "Thank you."

He waved his finger. "Not me. This is from Lena, the mother of Koi. What you did for her was thoughtful." He tapped his hand against his chest where a pendant would be. "She wants to make peace with you."

I grimaced. "Does she blame me for his death?"

Shikoba clasped his hands. "We come from the old ways. Some of us have been around since before the white man came, when we were still fighting human tribes. We have seen many changes, but uninvited visitors have always made us uneasy, and for good reason. She does not want to anger the spirits by burying her son with hatred in her heart. When a child is murdered, all a mother seeks is justice. They will never have understanding or peace, so they look for someone to blame. If it hadn't been you, it would have been the storm. Or perhaps something else."

"Tell her thank you." I didn't know what else to say. *Sorry* seemed like an inadequate word for the tremendous loss of a child.

Shikoba glanced around the cabin. "You're safe here. The lights in the house will stay on so it looks occupied. Don't step outside," he cautioned. "And don't let your wolf out."

"I know. Tak filled me in."

His eyes drifted upward. "A clear sky means Koi will have a good journey."

"You don't think he's already gone where he needs to go?"

"He's with his mother now. His spirit is trying to comfort her. It is our way of showing respect to the living when we die."

I set the basket down. "Safe journey."

Shikoba nodded, and I closed the door as he walked away.

"Melody? Wake up, lazybones."

I squinted, my vision blurred in the darkness as I tried to make sense of the shadow looming over me. "Lakota?" I eased up on my elbows. "What time is it?"

"After dark. My wolf went for a long run. The funeral is probably underway now, so I came back to check on you. I didn't see the lights on and thought you might have taken off."

I chuckled softly. "There's no electricity, so I lit a few candles. I just closed my eyes for a minute."

"You fell asleep with the window open," he said gruffly. Lakota stepped away and lit a second candle. "The wind must have blown out the candles."

Yawning, I stretched my sore muscles. "I thought you changed your mind and went with them."

He set the yellow candle on the windowsill and closed the shutters. "I'm not family. I knew Koi, but it would confuse his spirit to see me. Especially if he saw the truth of why I'm here."

I sat up, my feet touching the floor. "You don't really believe all that, do you?"

He knelt before the fireplace and lit a third candle, then a fourth. "Why shouldn't I? Both sides of my family tell many stories, and I compare them to what I've heard from elders on some of my travels. There's got to be some truth to it. The spirit goes somewhere. Can you imagine how hard it would be to leave behind your family? You've heard of Gravewalkers. They can see the dead." He stood up and placed a fifth candle on the mantel. "Maybe seeing strangers would confuse your spirit and make you stay and protect your family. If that's even a remote possibility, I don't want to damn Koi's spirit to limbo."

"I'm going to stay and haunt you, Lakota Cross."

He turned on his heel, his eyes sharp. "Don't say things like that."

My stomach fluttered. "I'm just kidding."

Looking at Lakota in a pair of jeans reminded me that I still had on my towel.

"Here." He tossed me a pile of fabric. "It was outside your door along with two bottles of water."

I lifted the lightweight material. Someone had left me a brown nightshirt that reached my knees. It had a V-neck collar with crisscross laces. While Lakota lit a few more candles, I pulled the shirt over my head and stood up, the towel dropping to the floor. "Fits perfect. I feel so guilty that they did all this for me."

"Did what?"

I gestured to the basket. "They also brought me food."

Curiosity flickered in his eyes. "You must have made an impression on them."

I decided not to mention the necklace. "You can eat if you're hungry. I don't mind."

"You didn't eat?" He lifted the basket and then sat in front of the hearth, placing everything on the rug. "Let's see what we've got here. Flatbread, peppers, tomatoes, butter, jerky, blueberries, a slice of pie—most of this was harvested on their land. Except for maybe the pie. The elders don't trust what humans are selling these days; it's not natural. A lot of indigenous human tribes have gotten diseases since they began eating processed food. Obviously that won't affect Shifters, but they prefer to live off the land as much as possible. Did you see their garden on the west side of the property?"

I shook my head.

"It's big. I'd like to have something like that someday." Lakota drew up one knee and folded a piece of bread. "I should light a fire."

The air did have a slight chill.

I got up and hefted a log. "Will one be enough to keep you toasty warm?"

He laughed with a mouthful of bread. "I'm not cold, Freckles. It's just too dark in here. Feels like I'm in your brothers' backyard fort. Is that rickety old thing still standing?"

When the kindling crackled to life, I sat on the hearth. "As long as that pack has children, the fort will stand."

Lakota tore off a strip of bread and used it to spread butter on the larger piece before offering it to me. A flush of warmth went through my body when his finger brushed against mine. It seemed like such an innocuous gesture, and I couldn't figure out why I was having that reaction every time we touched. Maybe it was my wolf responding to the idea of someone feeding me.

"How's your ass?" He gave me a one-sided grin.

I opened my mouth, uncertain if I'd heard him correctly.

Lakota pinched a few blackberries from a bowl. "I bet you're sore from the long ride back."

"Oh. That. It wasn't so bad. Tak kept me company."

A peculiar look flashed across his face, and he patted the spot beside him. "The rug's nice and soft."

"Okay."

After putting the fireplace screen in place, I stood up and sat next to him on the rug. The log snapped a few times as the flames intensified. The warmth was immediate, the luminous glow sublime. I washed down the bread with a gulp of water and tasted the blackberries. The food was alive, awakening my taste buds to natural flavors that weren't processed and hosed down with chemicals. It made me feel more connected to this place—to these people.

"You look good without makeup," he said.

I combed my hair with my fingers. "I look like a mess is what I look like. No hair dryer."

"I like my women a little on the wild side," he said with a wink. Lakota leaned back on his elbows and glanced at the plate between us. "You'd better eat that pie."

"They forgot the silverware."

"Indulge me."

When he licked his lips, it was so sensual that memories of our kiss flashed through my mind. Lakota had nice lips, the kind every woman dreamed about tasting. His hair had fallen away from his face, allowing the contours of his jaw to stand out. But it wasn't his jaw or even his lips that I was looking at. His arresting eyes burned as hot as the flames in the fireplace.

I picked off a piece of the crust with my fingers.

"That's a sad little bite," he mused. "Since when is Melody Cole afraid to get her hands dirty? I remember a girl who once climbed to the top of a telephone pole on a dare."

"And who's the one that started it?" I reminded him. "I also recall the fire department coming to get me down."

He threw back his head and laughed. "You threatened to pee on my head if I came up after you. What choice did I have? Hope didn't want to get us in trouble by calling the pack. Anyhow, the firemen seemed tickled by it."

"Oh, I'm sure. Having to get the ladder and rescue a girl from the top of a pole must have been the highlight of their day. They wanted to know what I was doing up there."

"What did you tell them?"

I licked my finger. "That I wanted to make a call."

We both erupted in laughter, and Lakota fell onto his back.

When he settled down, I set the pie plate on his chest. "You deserve this more than I do. That wolf back there wanted to kill me. If you hadn't reacted when you did—"

"Don't sell yourself short. Your arrow probably saved us, so we're even." Lakota lifted the wedge of pie, and two peach slices splattered onto his chest. He shoved what was left into his mouth, his cheeks as fat as a chipmunk's.

I set the empty plate in the basket and moved it out of the way. "I hope you realize they didn't bring us napkins."

Lakota smiled as he swallowed the pie, and my eyes dragged down to the peach slices on his pec. "Waste not, want not. My people believe in sharing."

I flicked his arm with my finger. "I know *all* about your people, and I don't seem to recall your stepfather serving your mother dinner on his chest."

He licked his thumb. "You never came over after midnight."

Not one to turn down a dare, I leaned over and wrapped my mouth around a piece of fruit and ate it. Then I swirled my tongue around the sticky spot on his chest to lick off the juice.

Lakota sucked in a sharp breath, his response immediate. His pupils dilated as he watched with a look of surprise, and his entire body tensed beneath my touch.

Before I could sit back, he cupped his hand behind my neck and locked eyes with me. "Do that again," he whispered. His hand softened its hold, his fingers petting my hair.

I leaned over, my eyes still on his, and devoured the last piece. He watched my mouth as I licked my lips, his chest rising and falling with each hurried breath. It saddened me that at such a young age, he'd made the decision to distance himself from women. That he'd never had a woman show him how desirable he was or make him feel alive with a sensual stroke of her finger, like what mine was doing with the peach juice around his hardened nipple. I'd never had a man react this way to my touch—as if he craved nothing else. Lakota had denied himself affection, and he was starved for it.

Even though he was lying submissively beneath me, his raw power vibrated, awakening my wolf. Now that I'd seen him in battle, I knew how expertly he could flip a man over and take his life.

Lakota cradled my neck in his hands, his gaze roving from my mouth up to my messy hair. He chuckled, his eyes twinkling with humor.

"Maybe this isn't such a good idea. Neither of us can be serious." I tried to move, but he pinned me against him.

"No, it's not that."

"Then what?"

He touched a lock of my hair. "I was just imagining what my adoptive parents would think of me bringing home a girl with purple hair."

My heart raced, and I quickly sat up and quenched my dry throat with half a bottle of water. Was he actually implying that he wanted to bring me home to meet his family?

Lakota rolled to his side. "What's wrong?"

"It's... it's just hot in here. Maybe we should put out the fire."

His hand grazed across my bare thigh. "Maybe I don't want to put out the fire."

CHAPTER 13

LAKOTA LIFTED ME INTO HIS arms and held me close. Instead of moving straight to the bed, he looked deep into my eyes as he stood in the center of the room. "I've never met a more courageous female."

For the first time in my life with Lakota, I didn't have a comeback. I felt swept away, no longer confused about what I wanted—what my wolf wanted. As he carried me to the bed, I placed my hand over his heart. The rhythm was strong and picking up speed.

Strangely, I was more nervous than I'd ever been with a man. Was I going to have to take charge and show him what to do? Being given someone's virginity was a profound honor, and I wasn't sure if I deserved that privilege.

When he placed me on the bed and ran his hands up my bare thighs and sensually caressed my hips, I realized that Lakota was a sexual creature who required little guidance. He didn't need to ask me what I liked—my body told him.

Gripping the pillow behind my head, I gasped from the heat of his mouth against my bare skin, his teeth nipping and tongue tasting below my navel.

Lakota's eyes widened, and he froze. "Are you okay?"

I nodded, my voice falling to a whisper. "I'm just a little nervous."

He climbed over me and rested half his body on mine.

"How do you think I feel? It's only the most memorable experience of my life." Lakota kissed the tip of my nose. "No pressure."

I laughed softly and relaxed. "Are you sure you want this? Want me?"

His eyes hooded, and he touched his lips to mine, drawing in a deep breath. "I love the way you smell." His hips rocked against mine, and I sucked in a sharp breath. "The way you feel." He kissed me, his lips trailing down to my neck. "The way you taste."

I was certain I was trembling beneath him, my nails scoring his back.

"Come on," he said, sitting up and pulling me onto his lap.

Straddling him, I delivered a molten kiss. Our tongues teased each other, barely touching yet daring the other to go deeper. Lakota might have had no experience in bed, but he'd clearly mastered the art of kissing, taking it to a whole new level. It was a slow kiss, the kind you feel all the way down to your toes—the kind that left no uncertainty about where that moment was heading.

Lakota lifted the hem of my nightshirt and tossed the garment onto the floor. My nipples tightened beneath his gaze. No man had ever looked at me the way he did. It was more than just physical admiration; it was as if he could see into my soul. He admired my small breasts with reverence, though he refrained from touching them.

He brushed his knuckles against my stomach, teasing me until my eyes hooded and I arched my back. Lakota slowly dragged his hand between my breasts, his fingertips awakening every nerve in my body as they moved up to my jaw. He stared amorously into my eyes, never blinking. My wolf stirred, begging for more affection.

"What are you looking at?"

He leaned forward so his breath warmed my lips. "Your wolf. She's watching me."

A tingle turned into a power surge as I rocked my hips. Lakota brushed his thumb across my bottom lip, so I took it into my mouth and sucked. He reclined his head, his breath heavy and eyes closed. His restraint was palpable, and it felt as if I were mounted on a rodeo bull before the gate opened.

I took his hand and led it down to my breast. When I rocked my hips again, the urgency to mate with him tightened like a coil. Firelight held our bodies together, and shadows wrapped around us like a blanket, desire fueling the flames.

He kissed me hard and held me tighter. My fingers tangled in his hair, and I clawed at his back.

"Mine," he whispered, his mouth moving to my ear.

Something shifted in that moment, something so deep within me that I almost felt myself split apart. Not desire, but love. It terrified me like the flames of a fire, yet I was drawn to it like a moth. I wanted to feel that warmth and never leave.

When I rose onto my knees, Lakota drew my nipple into his mouth and circled it with his tongue. Nothing was hurried or rough about his touch, but a moan was trapped deep in his throat. He savored me, tasted me, and admired me with every touch. I rested my hands on his broad shoulders while he took control, his mouth greedily latching onto my other breast, his hands splayed across my back. Lakota made me feel beautiful without saying a word.

"Are you sure you're new at this?" I asked on a breath.

His eyes met mine. I'd never really looked at them up close. A thin circle of ebony rimmed both irises, and the blue glittered like pale gemstones with numerous facets. "On my word, Melody Cole. You're the only one."

Only one. Those two words lingered in my head for longer than they should have.

Lakota turned us around and lay down on his back, me on top. It was then that I realized he was constantly shifting so that I had the dominant position. Maybe he wanted me to take charge, but I had a feeling he was still afraid of his assertiveness when it came to women. Lakota was truly the most handsome man I'd ever known, and I suddenly realized the honor he was giving me. He could have given himself to *anyone*. Someone more beautiful, more experienced, a stranger, even one of his old girlfriends back in Austin who might have been holding out for him. I stroked his jaw, knowing he'd made the choice because he trusted me.

When Lakota reached down to unbutton his pants, I stopped him and got off the bed. I stood before him, taking measured care to remove his pants and treat him like a prince.

A blush reddened his cheeks, and he averted his eyes. That was the only moment I'd seen a flicker of uncertainty. No woman had ever seen his body. Not like this. Hoping to erase any doubts he might have, I placed a kiss by his navel. My right hand explored the fine hairs on his legs, tracing up to the soft skin between his thighs before stroking his shaft.

He bucked beneath my touch, his body arching in a magnificent display. I kept touching him so he would get used to someone else's hand on his body. I remembered my first time and how I was a trembling mess, so I wanted him to feel relaxed. His energy throbbed against me, the power of his wolf undeniable.

When I bent over and kissed his Adam's apple, a deep groan vibrated against my lips. His musky scent was in my nose, the salt from his skin on my tongue as I licked the base of his throat and then nipped his chin.

"I like these games you play," he said. "Lie on top of me so I can feel your weight."

I eased myself over him until our bodies were flush. It took every ounce of willpower not to rise and take him inside me.

Lakota's fingertips grazed my cheeks. "I don't want this to be rushed. You deserve my attention."

"Do whatever feels right."

He softly kissed my mouth. "This isn't about me; it's about *us*. You… and me."

"Stop saying that," I said, my voice quavering.

"Saying what?"

"You, me, us."

He rolled me onto my side, his back to the fire. "That's all there is. Listen. Do you hear the silence outside our window? No crickets singing, no owls, no airplanes, no people. The world disappeared, and we're all that's left."

My breath caught when his hand eased between my legs, his eyes never straying from mine. I clutched the back of his neck as he pleasured me slowly, our skin melting together like porcelain against bronze.

"It's softer than I thought," he murmured.

My Shifter instincts were making me want to turn my back to him and feel him behind me, but instead I bent one leg at the knee so he could know the pleasure elicited from his touch.

Dark, unquenchable desire pooled in his eyes. When I sucked in a sharp breath and made a whimpering moan, he quickly stopped.

"Am I hurting you?"

I kissed him hard, nipping on his bottom lip and then guiding his mouth to my neck as I grew wetter. Lakota sucked on my neck, and a split second later, he reached down and hooked my leg over his hip.

"Please, take me," I whispered. "*Please.*"

He stroked the head of his shaft along my slick entrance, and it nearly split me apart. "This feels too good. I don't know if I can control my wolf. Maybe we should stop."

I knew exactly what he was afraid of. Lakota had never experienced the power and ancient heat that occurs when Shifters have sex. The animal within us comes alive, and their spirit flickers in our eyes.

"It's normal," I assured him. "It feels like you're going to shift, but you're not. Trust me. That's what intensifies the pleasure—makes us lose control. Don't fight it. Give in to your wolf."

Lakota suddenly rolled on top of me. "I need to be inside you," he growled, rocking his hips. It wasn't a discussion. He drove deep, the connection so insatiable that it was every bit as explosive as being in heat.

His chest swelled, and his eyes locked on mine. Lakota had finally become one with his animal spirit. He slammed his hips into mine again and again, and our bodies married. Lakota was everywhere—on top of me, inside me, in my thoughts, in my memories, his voice in my ear, his breath on my face, his taste on my tongue, and our souls joined.

Without warning, he abruptly stopped and sat back on his heels, an inscrutable expression on his face as he looked down at me.

"What's wrong? Why did you stop?"

"To see if I could," he admitted.

Rising onto my knees, I placed a tender kiss on his mouth. I couldn't begin to understand the conflicting emotions he must have been experiencing because of fears he'd carried his whole life.

Lakota needed to know without question that I wanted him, so I turned around on his lap, my back against his chest. He kissed my nape, his hands cupping my breasts.

His shaft was thick and hard like granite. But instead of satiating his needs, he reached down and slipped his fingers inside me. "Do you like this?" he asked, the deep timbre of his voice prickling the hairs on the back of my neck.

With each gasp I made, he repeated the action. I reached up and locked my arms around his neck, giving him all of me. He pulled his fingers out and quickly circled them around my sweet spot until I whimpered. When I couldn't hold on any longer, I fell forward on my hands and knees.

"Now," I urged him.

Lakota branded me, burying himself deep as he fell across my back. "I don't want to stop," he said, his voice ragged.

"*Don't stop.*"

Two words he needed to hear.

Permission.

Invitation.

I clawed the pillow, my inner wolf forcing her wildness into me as I rode out his demanding thrusts.

Lakota pressed between my shoulder blades, coaxing me to lie flat on my stomach. He stopped, his body feverish as the weight of him bore down on me. "Not like that. Too out of control."

With his heart thumping against my back, he slowly rocked into me. Lakota's rhythm changed to one that was deep and purposeful, forcing me to take every inch of him—his weight, his breath, his heat, his moans, and especially where our bodies joined. He touched places inside me, and I couldn't get enough of him.

"*Mine,*" he whispered.

Pleasure tore through me like a bolt of lightning. I tossed the pillow onto the floor and rested my head against the mattress. Lakota placed his hands over mine, and we locked fingers. That single gesture made me feel more connected to him than anything else. I tilted my hips, my climax speeding out of control. I came hard, clenching around him so tightly that he growled. Lakota suddenly flipped me over, and I stared up at him breathlessly.

His eyes were like ice as he plunged into me in search of his release. "I want to see your face when I come."

And I wanted to see his. The longer I stared into his eyes, the deeper I fell, and the more passionate he became. Ancient heat coursed in Lakota's veins, and he finally succumbed to his animal instincts. His rhythm was hard and fast, knocking the bed against the wall. I craved him, needed him. When I locked my ankles around his waist, he stiffened and roared as he came.

I trembled beneath the passing storm, my hands resting on Lakota's sweaty shoulders. His arms gave way, and he fell on top of me, out of breath. I didn't complain or try to wriggle free, even though he'd smothered me with his full weight. It was a beautiful moment for a man who, at the age of thirty, finally knew what it was like to be completely lost and found all at once.

He began kissing my shoulder.

"Is the big bad wolf going to eat me now?" I quipped.

Still inside me, he looked up and gave me a wolfish grin. "I just might."

I wanted to stay that way, but Lakota slowly rolled onto his side. With his back to the wall, he leaned against it to give me more room and propped his head in his hand.

He circled his finger around my breast, and I shivered, goose pimples erupting across my skin at the sudden loss of his body heat.

"Was it what you thought it would be?" I asked.

He threaded back his hair, which was tangled and slightly damp. "Not exactly. It was…"

"What?"

He shook his head. "I don't want to sound foolish."

"I won't judge. Promise," I said, crossing my heart with two swipes of my finger.

His brow furrowed as if he thought he was going to regret opening his mouth. "It was… wetter than I thought it would be."

I chuckled. "That's a good thing. That's when you know that you're doing it right."

He stroked his hand across my midsection, seemingly mesmerized by the way my body responded to his touch. "And would you say that I did it right?"

I placed my hand on his. "It scares me how good you were. You're going to have quite the reputation once the women back home find out what they've been missing."

"That remains to be seen," he said obliquely. "Come here and lie in my arms, female."

He held up his left arm, and I folded into his embrace. It felt comforting and safe to snuggle against him—to nuzzle my face into his neck. I loved that part more than I would ever admit to him.

"Is this what it's always like?" he asked.

I wanted to say no, because I'd never had a man hold me after sex, not like this. But I shrugged my answer, deciding to take the silent route.

The promise I'd extracted at the motel ran through my mind. Maybe Lakota had already forgotten, but I couldn't stop thinking about it as we held each other. I'd asked him to be open to the idea of sex with someone he liked, and his reply kept repeating in my mind: *"The next woman my heart beats fast for, I'll invite her to my bed."*

Did his heart beat fast for me?

Lakota stroked my hair, his eyes drawn to the fire. "I don't think I'll ever be right about my father's crime, but it's not holding me back anymore, and I have you to thank for that."

I shifted to look up at him. "You are *not* your father's son."

Lakota closed his eyes. "I know that now."

"What's upsetting you?"

He pressed a kiss to my forehead. "I finally understand how vulnerable a woman is—how much trust she gives to a man. I wish he were alive so I could kill him myself. A second-in-command, violating the trust of a girl who looked up to him. It fucking burns me to know he did that. I hope his dark spirit is pressed to the ashes of the underworld."

A chill ran through me, and he held me tighter.

"Do you miss your family up north?"

"Sometimes. But I can see or talk to them anytime on the computer or the phone."

I drew an invisible heart on his chest. "Do you think someday you'll return to live closer to them?"

Lakota wouldn't be a bounty hunter forever. Would he want to join a pack? Did he consider Austin or Cognito his home? Where would he go?

"My home will be where my heart is, and that depends on who I give it to."

"Do you see yourself in a pack or doing something else? Do you dream about the city or country life? I feel like I don't know that much about you. We never had deep conversations before."

He rubbed the corner of his mouth. "I don't know. I would rather be in a pack, but I'd have to trust the Packmaster enough to give him my loyalty. I'll probably have to get mated."

I snorted. "Why?"

His fingertips circled around my back. "I think seeing so many happy couples around me would make it hard to do my job as second-in-command. I would want a mate to talk to late at night about the things I couldn't tell the pack."

"Maybe you just need a best friend."

"Isn't that what a mate is supposed to be?"

I brushed my finger around the fine hairs on his chest. "How did someone like you become such a romantic?"

A moment skipped by before he answered. "Maybe I was just born to love since I wasn't conceived in it."

"You've done great things. You just don't realize it."

"It's my job. I help people. That's what I do."

But I wasn't talking about his job. Lakota had been the force that brought two families together. His very existence had healed his mother's pain—that much, I was certain of. He could have rejected her for giving him up, but as far back as I could remember, Lakota had always treated her like a second mom. He'd been Hope's protective big brother, and I couldn't imagine her having gone through life without his counsel. He was as kind as he was strong, and if he didn't think that was great, then he was blind.

He tucked one of my tresses behind my ear. "Can I ask you something?"

"I'm an open book. Except for chapter twelve."

Lakota held the pensive look on his face. "Has any man ever hurt you?"

I furrowed my brow. "I don't do relationships, remember? No broken hearts, just a bunch of yelling."

He tilted my chin up. "That's not what I meant. Has a

man ever... you know, *hurt* you? Is that the real reason why you don't get serious?"

I lowered my gaze to his lips. "My pack did a good job looking out for me, and I guess I was lucky with the men I dated. My relationship status has nothing to do with an abusive past. Your first assumptions back at the motel are correct. I don't get serious because I've got too much on my plate. I guess that makes me selfish."

He pressed his lips to my forehead. "I don't think you're selfish at all."

We fell into silence again, and my heart clenched at the idea that he cared enough to ask.

"Does it ever get lonely on the road?"

"Sometimes." After a thoughtful pause, his voice was rougher yet firm. "If you ever need me for anything, I'll come. If you're ever in trouble, if you ever need my help, I'll come for you. Do you understand what I'm saying? You're not just a friend of the family to me. Not anymore."

"You shouldn't make promises you can't keep. Things change. People change."

"I don't care if you're mated with children. None of that matters. My loyalty is a lifetime offer. On my word, I'll come for you."

Wolves by nature are loyal to the ones they love—to those they consider family. I'd known wolves who'd forged bonds, but their human sides didn't get along at all. It was an honor for Lakota to offer that kind of unbending loyalty. I shared that same connection with Hope, but this was different somehow, though I wasn't sure why.

"Lakota," I whispered, but his name sounded more like a prayer on my lips.

He lowered his chin. "Did you say something?"

"No. Just breathing."

"Can you do me a favor?"

I peered up at him. "It depends. If it involves a telephone pole, your answer is no."

"Will you rub my back? I think I pulled a muscle in my shoulder."

Grinning impishly, I said, "I'm great with my hands."

"Oh yeah? Prove it."

After they had cleaned themselves up and chugged down a bottle of water, Lakota received the most pleasurable massage of his entire life. Melody sat astride his back and pressed the heels of her small hands into his shoulders, working her way down at a glorious pace. He loved the feel of her touch, how gentle and forceful her hands could be, and he smiled against the pillow when she rubbed the backs of his thighs. But his smile melted away as he became amorous once again. As much as he wanted to give in to those feelings, he didn't. He had already known her in that way, and now he wanted to know her more intimately.

Melody sought comfort in his arms for close to an hour while they talked. He listened to her stories, some of which he'd heard before from his sister. Lakota liked hearing her version—she was a captivating storyteller. Not once did they reminisce over their childhood. Instead, they filled in the gaps of their time apart and pondered an uncertain future. Not just the immediate future but also what life held in store for each of them years down the road. Melody said she hoped that one day her boutique would flourish enough to become a chain, and she liked the idea of possibly traveling or living somewhere else for a while, especially after Lakota had talked about some of the places he'd been. He mentioned wanting twenty kids, just to make her laugh. She wished him luck finding a willing mate.

It made Lakota wonder what kind of woman he was looking for. Melody had drive and creativity as well as a sense of humor—all the best parts a man could hope for in a woman. He was beside himself. *Who exactly is this unspeakably beautiful female in my arms, and why hasn't she fled from me and my shameful past?*

As he cradled her close, Lakota knew exactly what he and his wolf wanted: to protect her. He was usually wary around women, yet being with Melody felt so natural and easy.

He'd never imagined having such strong feelings for another wolf. When he was growing up, only one other Shifter lived in the house. Lakota's family loved him unconditionally, and love transcended Breed or politics. The animalistic Chitah traits of his adoptive father had rubbed off on him. He mirrored their actions and understood why they protected their family with their lives. Even though he was in good standing with the Shifters in Austin, he'd never imagined that anyone would consider him a catch. His unusual living circumstances generated much gossip, and he wondered if his inexperience with packs might even hinder his chances of ever joining one. Packmasters were very selective, and he was still learning all the nuances of their ways.

Seeming half-asleep, Melody murmured against his chest, "Lakota?"

Hearing his name spoken in such a fragile voice made his wolf stir. "Yes?"

"Remember what you said about my hair and your parents?"

He had to stop and think before he recalled the conversation in which he'd joked about what his adoptive parents' reaction might be to him dating a girl with violet hair. "Yes. Why?"

When she breathed heavily, he nudged her awake.

"What will your mother and Lorenzo think?" she murmured.

"Of your hair?"

Melody shook her head. "That I'm not like you."

Lakota pressed a kiss to her head. He wanted to say it didn't matter. To him it didn't. But his mother and stepfather had always assured him that one day he would find a girl who belonged to his tribe, and they would settle in a pack. Maybe it didn't matter which tribe, so long as his bloodline would carry on the traditions of the Native people.

While he had made the comment only in jest, Melody's mind must have been working overtime in her sleep. Was she afraid that both families would shun her for different reasons? Family was important to Shifters. Family was everything.

Most of all, he wondered if her doubts meant that she *wanted* to get serious. It was all so sudden—too sudden.

"*Shhh.*" Lakota began to hum an ancient lullaby. He thought he felt a tear roll down his chest, but he never saw it. He didn't like that other men had thrown her away. It had somehow jaded her and made her less receptive to the idea of soul mates. And that mattered to him—she deserved nothing less.

For a time, he played with the soft locks of her hair, noticing the dark roots beneath. Melody had always respected their traditions and honored them. She was devoted to her family, had a courageous wolf, and possessed a giving nature. Beneath the mismatched clothes, pale skin, and colorful hair was a woman with roots that threaded deep into his soul. He wasn't sure what would grow from it, but he felt the change just as surely as he felt the beating of her heart.

Once Melody was finally asleep, he sat up and watched her. She was breathtakingly beautiful and reminded him of a nymph or a fairy. Melody had always been assertive and strong, but she also possessed a purity and a femininity that captivated him. Her big green eyes would sparkle whenever she looked up at him, and he loved the way her mind worked. Lakota admired her soft curves, the shape of her breasts, and how her freckles captured the story of a little girl who'd spent her summers chasing butterflies in open fields.

As he reached down for a blanket, he noticed scars on her foot. He blinked at them for a moment before remembering the wolf attack during the Shifter war long ago. Strangely, in all the years since, he'd never noticed them when she ran around barefoot. Looking at them, he remembered her unbending loyalty to protecting her pack, the way he'd practically had to rope her to his horse to keep her from going back to fight alongside them. Those were the marks of a true warrior.

Lakota placed a kiss along the scars and covered her with the blanket. He fluffed a pillow and put it behind her head. She was a heavy sleeper, and as her eyelids fluttered, he wondered what she was dreaming.

After setting a glass of water on the bedside table, he collected the bowls and plates from the rug and placed them inside the basket. The leftover bread and beef jerky would be a sufficient breakfast, so he wrapped them tightly in a napkin and left them on the table on the opposite side of the room.

He cracked open a window to let in a cool breeze. Not wanting to lose the heat from the fire, Lakota poked the log until the embers glowed and a small flame reignited. It was tempting to return to the bed and fall asleep next to her, then possibly wake up to make love again, but another instinct was taking hold—one he could neither control nor contain.

Lakota shifted and settled down beside the bed to guard her. The instinct to guard this female was stronger than anything he'd ever known, and the compulsion for his wolf to hunt for her was growing. Not enough to leave her alone, but it made him wonder what it meant. That was a gesture shared only between life mates.

He put the thought of hunting rabbits out of his mind and gazed upon the fire. Maybe it wasn't wise to get so attached to a free spirit. Fated lovers didn't always have a happy ending.

When something brushed against his back, he swung his head around. Melody's arm was hanging over the side of the bed, her fingers lost in his silver fur. Lakota growled approvingly, the thrumming sound vibrating against her hand. He licked her fingers to let her know he was there and that she could sleep soundly while under his watch. It felt right and familiar. As he began to slip away, his wolf stood up and leapt onto the bed to curl up beside her.

Lakota wasn't sure what the fates had in store for them, but he knew one thing—his wolf was willing to die for Melody.

CHAPTER 14

"I'M COMING!" I SLIPPED INTO my nightshirt and ran my fingers through my tousled hair.

The sharp knocks sounded again, and I squinted when the cabin door opened and sunlight slapped me in the face.

Tak leaned against the doorjamb, the sun shining on the tattooed side of his face. "Have you seen Lakota?"

"No."

He smiled so wide it made me uneasy. "Funny. I could have sworn he would be in here."

"That's presumptuous."

"He can't sleep under our roof, and he knows better than to run the grounds during a burial. So..." Tak peered around me.

I opened the door and stepped back. "Look for yourself. He's not here, unless I somehow managed to stuff the Big Bad Wolf into that basket."

Tak scratched his jaw and studied the picnic basket by the door. "White men tell horrifying stories to their children. What do you call them?" He snapped his fingers. "Ah yes. Fairy tales. Did you ever hear the one about those wicked children who ate a woman's house and then shoved her in the oven?"

I folded my arms. "Was there something you wanted?"

"I'm heading out and thought Lakota might want to come along."

"What about all the brouhaha going on with the locals?"

Tak strode over to the table and pilfered a piece of jerky. He stood so tall that his head nearly touched the ceiling. "We had a few scouts check out the roads this morning. Looks like the Council stepped in and made them leave before the state police came to check it out. Not my concern anymore."

I glanced outside. "What time is it?"

"Almost two."

I waited for him to laugh and tell me it was a joke, but he didn't. *Did I really sleep the entire morning?* Covering my face with one hand, I sat in the chair.

"You're free to go," he added, licking his thumb.

"Is everyone back from the burial?"

He widened his stance and scratched his neck. "I just woke up from a shift. Some are resting, I think. I can smell food cooking in the kitchen. The mood is lighter today. The elders say the sunshine is a good omen."

I drank a sip of water from a bottle. "Except for the fact that a murderer is still out there."

"Yes, but it's no longer your concern."

"It might be."

He gnawed on his jerky. "How so?"

"It occurred to me that if the cops return to the crime scene, they're going to wonder about all the fresh blood and my clothes. A lot of people saw me in those pants. They're memorable."

Tak strode toward the door. "You needn't worry about that. I went back this morning before dawn, and your clothes were gone. So was the blood. Whichever rogue pack those wolves belonged to must have tidied things up. I'll see if I can find something your size."

"I don't want to take anything else from your tribe. Your belt will do."

He arched an eyebrow. Tak slowly unbuckled his belt and

slid it out of his pant loops. After he flung it on the table, he
headed out.

I steered my gaze around the empty room and let it linger
on the bed, visions of last night's lovemaking appearing like
a phantom dream. Funny how lifeless and hollow the cabin
seemed without Lakota's larger-than-life personality. The last
thing I remembered was falling asleep in his arms. By the
looks of it, he'd cleaned up and erased all evidence of him
having been here.

It was foolish to think we would wake up in each other's
arms, but a sliver of me desired it. My feelings for Lakota were
changing, and it caught me off guard. People just didn't fall
in love that quickly. It had to be the sex talking, and I needed
to get my head together and distance myself from this place.

Tak's belt fit around my waist loosely, but at least with the
long shirt it looked like an ensemble I could get away with
wearing in the summertime.

My hopes of closing a deal with Shikoba were dashed. The
man had just buried one of his packmates, and the last thing
he needed was some stranger badgering him.

I made the bed, tidied up the cabin, and collected my
purse before heading out. Instead of entering the main house,
I circled around the side toward the front. The gravel hurt my
feet, and the two men sitting on the front porch sipped their
cold beers and watched with mild interest. When I reached
my Jeep and opened the door, I noticed the keys weren't there.

"Shit." I set my purse on the seat and headed for the house.
"Do you know where my keys are?"

One of them jerked his thumb at the door.

Before I could knock, both men abruptly set their bottles
down and rose to their feet. There was nothing casual about
it, and it made me turn around to see what had captured their
attention. A silver car was heading toward us down the private
road, dust kicking up behind it.

A cacophony of shouts and footfalls sounded from within
the house as the pack became aware that visitors were on the

property. I hid behind a wooden beam, uncertain what was unfolding before me. Kaota appeared and descended the steps, but instead of going out to greet the visitors, he stopped, his arms folded and a stony look on his face.

Two men exited the vehicle. One of them was a husky man with an anemic complexion and thinning hair the color of wheat. He squinted at the sunlight and dabbed a white handkerchief across his broad forehead.

The driver smoothed out his bushy mountain-man beard. His brown boots kicked around gravel as he approached Kaota at a leisurely pace. "I'm here to see Shikoba," he said, his accent hinting that he'd lived around these parts for a long time.

Kaota's voice fell flat. "He's in mourning. What's your business on our land, Robert?"

The bearded man took off his mirrored sunglasses and tucked them into his shirt pocket. "Jack and I came out here to have a conversation. Word is you've got a problem with your tribe."

"We've got no problems."

"And the dead boy?"

"That's *your* problem," Kaota bit out. "You're the big man on the Council. What are you going to do to protect our rights?"

Robert scratched his head. "Word out there ain't good, Kaota. People are sayin' your tribe had something to do with the murders. I'd hate to find out there's a cover-up happening right beneath my nose."

Kaota stepped forward. "Did Koi's death look like a suicide? Did the girl rise up from the dead and tear open his jugular?"

Stroking his beard, Robert said, "No, but someone slit that girl's throat and stabbed her in the abdomen. Now, I'm not making any accusations, but it looks like maybe Koi and the girl were secret lovers, and one of your people found out and decided to teach them both a lesson."

"And what of *your* people?" Kaota fired back. "Are they incapable of murder?"

Robert widened his stance. "Look, we're only here to discuss what everyone else is talking about. If Koi *did* shift to protect her, we would have found his clothes on the scene. But we didn't."

"And what does that prove?"

"It leads us to believe one of two things. Either Koi stalked and attacked her, and they fought to the death, or Koi met up with her, and someone in your tribe caught them together. An outside Shifter committing the crime wouldn't have stolen his clothes if he wanted to pin it on Koi. From *his* perspective, stealing the clothes would make it seem like someone else was there, and Koi had to shift to protect her. Make sense? Killers want to cover their tracks, not leave breadcrumbs."

"And you think we're stupid?"

Robert sighed and shook his head. "Comments like that make me wonder. They found a knife by the body but no clothes. All I can do is look at the facts and see who had motive. If someone in your tribe was the culprit, then his motive ain't gonna be to pin it on the tribe. He probably acted on impulse. Who knows, maybe I've got it all wrong. Maybe the killer was attacking the girl, and Koi's wolf was close enough that he heard the screams. The thing is, I've worked out all the logical scenarios, and the one that *doesn't* make sense is one of the local Shifters having something to do with it. Not given the evidence we have, which is more than a missing pile of clothes. I can promise you that."

I gripped the beam while peering around the side. A gust of wind lifted my hair and caught Jack's attention.

The pasty man narrowed his eyes. "Who's she?"

My stomach knotted when Jack kept staring. Part of me wanted to ask for an escort out of town, but I didn't know either of those guys, and I had a feeling my best interests weren't their top priority at the moment. With Lakota's truck gone, I remained quiet.

"What do you want?" Kaota pressed.

Robert flicked a glance my way but kept his attention on Kaota. "We can't make arrests just yet, but it doesn't look good. I think you have a bad apple in your bunch, and Koi was in the wrong place at the wrong time with the wrong woman. If you know who's responsible, I'm asking that you turn him over. Disobey the law and suffer the consequences."

The door opened, and Shikoba came out. He knocked his cane angrily against the wood as he took his time descending each step. When he reached Kaota, he put his hand on his nephew's shoulder. Kaota reluctantly turned away and came up the porch.

"Koi is innocent," Shikoba informed Robert.

Robert nodded, his voice friendlier. "I know."

Shikoba looked up at a hawk circling overhead. "I remember one winter when your mother fell ill. She was a breath away from meeting her creator."

"I've heard the story."

"She carried you in her belly, and none of your people knew how to ease her suffering. With great reluctance, your father came to see me. I could have turned him away, but what would that say about my character? I decided if the child was meant to live, maybe he would do good things for us. There had to be a reason the spirits put me in charge of your lives."

Robert's eyes were downcast, and he scraped his heel against the ground. "We just want this to stop. The killer is getting more unpredictable, and that puts all of us at risk." He swung his gaze up, his eyes resolute. "You need to nip this in the bud, or we'll have no choice but to take action and seize your land. The laws out here state that only concrete evidence can get you imprisoned, but if we suspect you're covering up a crime, we have the right to evict suspects from the territory. People are demanding it."

"You are the Council. Demand order."

"Dammit, Shikoba. You know it doesn't work like that. I've got two packs knocking on my door, threatening to take matters into their own hands. Jack and I have been doing everything we can to put out the fire and keep them calm, but I don't reckon I can keep people from coming out here and seeking their own justice. *Their* women are the ones getting killed, and every one of them was linked to one of your men. Regardless of how divided everyone is, that kind of thing has always gone on. People just keep the affairs private so they don't have to deal with the scandal and shame of it all."

Shikoba straightened his back. "I am not so naive as to think someone in my tribe couldn't be guilty. But you must also accept that one of your own could be the demon in our midst. As leaders, we are responsible for keeping the peace—we must set the example. Our people look to us for wisdom. Don't let the herd drive the horseman."

Robert appeared to be buckling beneath the weight of public pressure to do something, yet he seemed like a man who wanted to do the right thing. His partner, Jack, leaned against the front of their car, arms crossed. Quiet didn't necessarily mean less powerful. The Councilmen were all equals, though usually one of them officiated more mating ceremonies and acted as the Council's representative.

"You have my word that I'll turn over anyone guilty of these crimes," Shikoba said. "But this land is sacred to us, so just know that if you try to move us out, we will have no choice but to go to war."

Robert shook his head. "Neither of us wants it to come to that. You and I have known each other a long time—all my life—and that's why I came out here. We chased off the men near the road who were planning to smoke you out. Most of them are the same people we deal with, and after the booze wears off, they'll go home. I don't want to convict a whole tribe for the crimes of one, but I'll have no choice if you're sheltering a killer. I've gotta do what I've gotta do to keep this whole thing from blowing up out of control. And if I find out you were the one who gave the order to kill those women to set some kind of example—"

"How dare you!" Kaota roared.

Shikoba swung his cane around to silence him.

Robert shifted his stance. "Who's the girl? I don't think I've ever seen a white woman on your land before." His eyes skated down to my bare feet and oversized belt. "Are you okay, honey?"

"I'm fine," I replied coolly.

He didn't look convinced.

Shikoba gave me a cursory glance. "She's with Lakota."

Clearly the truth would look even more suspect. Not many women drove up to do business with gemstone dealers and then wandered around their properties half naked.

"Lakota?" Robert stroked his beard. "Which one is that?"

"We also call him Sky Hunter."

Jack eased away from the car, his hands on his hips. "You mean the guy in the black pickup?" He scrunched his face and gave Robert a look I couldn't discern.

Shikoba squared his shoulders. "They're to be mated. Ceremony is tonight."

I stifled a laugh.

That seemed to satisfy Robert, and he motioned for Jack to get in the car. "Take my advice, Shikoba. Cooperate and hand over the killer. We'll be heading out now. If you hear any news, give me a call." He glanced around. "Do you have phones out here? Anyhow, I'll do what I can to keep the peace on my end, but I can't make any promises. We uphold the laws, not enforce them. We would have to call in Regulators of the Security Force, and they're not going to come out here and act as security guards. We'll talk more later."

Without another word, the two men got in the car and conversed for a few moments before driving away.

What other evidence did the Council have against the tribe? They seemed certain it was one of Shikoba's packmates, so they must have been keeping something else to themselves. If someone in the tribe had murdered Koi by accident, he would have panicked for sure. Koi was Shikoba's beloved nephew. Maybe the killer had taken the clothes because his scent was on them. I tried to imagine different scenarios, but detective work wasn't my forte.

Shikoba climbed the steps.

"You lied to him," I said. "About me and Lakota."

He turned and smiled. "It's only a lie if it doesn't happen."

CHAPTER 15

LAKOTA PULLED UP TO THE local Shifter bar and parked his truck at the back. When he'd woken up late that morning, he was lying naked on the floor. His wolf must have stayed up with her the whole night. Melody had slept through his shower, and he even stomped around loudly to rouse her before leaving. But she barely fluttered her eyelids, and he didn't have the heart to wake her. She looked so angelic, and he wanted to remember her that way. Since she was free to leave, maybe goodbyes would only make it harder for him to concentrate on the job at hand—the crime he still had to solve. After placing a chaste kiss on her forehead, he'd closed the door and headed to town to see what the word on the street was.

The first thing he'd done was swing by his apartment to change clothes and grab something to eat. He gassed up his truck, talked to a few people at the market, and finally headed over to the bar, where most of the gossip usually took place.

When he hopped out of the truck, he tied his hair up in a topknot and tucked his black skull T-shirt into his jeans to look less tribal. He wasn't as brown as the local tribes, his features were softer, and he didn't speak with the same intonation and dialect. Lakota knew very well how to tweak the way he spoke to different groups of people in order to blend in like a chameleon. Because of those factors, some of the locals were more relaxed around him.

The afternoon crowd was a slow one, with just a few regulars sitting at the bar. An old Patsy Cline song was playing on the jukebox while the local drunks watched a court show on TV.

Lakota eased up to the bar and ordered a cold one. Normally he drank in the back, but technically he didn't belong to the local tribes. The sign wasn't a hard rule so much as a means to keep order and prevent fights from breaking out. The bartender popped the lid off a bottle and set it on a coaster. Lakota remained standing, his forearm resting on the bar as he casually glanced up at the television.

He nodded to Red. "Any news on the murders?"

The slender man polished a glass, his mustache twitching and his eyes swinging up as he thought. "There was just a small mention at the end. The big story was the latest scandal with the mayor. Did ya hear about that one? Apparently *someone* got caught taking bribes. Just as well. We don't need all that media attention in our backyard. People like stickin' their noses where they don't belong." When a man at the end of the bar called for another beer, Red wiped his hand across his denim shirt. "Let me know if you want me to cook you up a burger."

Lakota stifled a laugh as the bartender wandered away. You needed an iron stomach to eat Red's food.

He took a slow sip from his bottle, reminiscing over the previous night with Melody, as he'd been doing all day. His first time had been so damn perfect, yet he couldn't help but wonder how he compared to her previous lovers. Maybe for her it hadn't been such a big deal, and that thought alone was enough to steal the wind from his sails.

"Woman trouble?" someone asked.

Lakota looked over his shoulder at the dark-haired man sitting in the booth close to him. He'd seen him in the bar a number of times. Kind of hard to miss a guy in blue cowboy boots, but people in small towns had their quirks.

The man swirled the alcohol in his glass, not looking up. "You just look like you've been struck by Cupid's motherfucking arrow."

"Isn't that why we're all here?" Lakota said conversationally.

"Amen," the man sang. "Are you one of *them*? You look familiar."

Lakota strode up to the booth and sat down so the man could get a good look at his eyes. "My father's white, so I pass for what matters."

"Good man," the stranger said. "My name's Crow."

"I'm Cross," Lakota said, using his surname. He casually lifted his bottle and gazed up at the TV again. "Are they saying who did it?"

Crow looked shitfaced. Four empty glasses were neatly lined against the wall, each with a wadded-up napkin stuffed inside.

"Someone should do something," a man grumbled from the bar. "Sick of this shit. Can't even let my daughter walk to her friend's house anymore."

Lakota decided not to fire off too many questions about the murder since people were listening. "Know of any job openings around here? I could use something steady."

Crow set down his glass and reached in his pocket. "Nope. Most Shifters around here live off what little land we got. A few guys haul lumber for good money, but they're pack bitches."

Quirking an eyebrow, Lakota asked, "What do you mean?"

"The packs have more money because they take all the good-paying jobs. The rest of us have to fend for ourselves." Crow opened a box of cigarettes and lit one. "Want a smoke?"

Lakota shook his head, studying the gold box of Pilgrims. "I quit last year. Too expensive."

Crow took a long drag. "You do what you gotta do." After the smoke cleared, he flicked his ashes into the ashtray. "So where's that woman you were with? You know, the one with the bubblegum hair."

"Don't know what you mean."

Crow exhaled smoke through his nostrils. "I drove around yesterday morning and saw you two outside the motel. I'm not judging. She's a sweet piece of ass."

Lakota shifted in his seat when he felt his wolf stirring with jealousy.

Crow finished off his drink and set the short glass on the napkin. "Pickings are slim around here. I guess you know that already. Grab on to what you can, or you'll end up with someone else's leftovers. Just between you and me, is she as wild in the sack as she looks?" He took a long drag from his cigarette, his gaze distant. "I sure do love a sweet face on a bad girl."

Lakota clenched his jaw. If Crow said one more word about Melody's sweet anything, he was going to get a thrashing. It was how a lot of men talked, but it felt too personal to hear someone speaking that way about someone he'd known his whole life.

Crow rested his elbows on the table and brushed his messy black hair away from his eyes. Then he gave Lakota a sardonic smile. "You may think you're fooling people with that little bun on your head and the shift in your accent, but at the end of the day, you're no different from the rest of them. Girls like her don't mess around with your kind, so I bet it felt real decadent taking a bite of forbidden fruit. Was she juicy?"

Lakota leaned forward, his voice low and menacing. "Do you feel that sharp prick between your legs?"

Crow looked down at where Lakota had his arm beneath the table with a blade to his groin. He took a puff of his cigarette and leveled Lakota with a stare. "Always knew you were all savages at heart. Just like that two-faced murderer."

"What are you talking about?"

Crow tapped a finger against his cheek. "Your buddy with the tats. I saw him running across my land on the night of the murders. Ask around. Other people have seen him wandering across territories where he doesn't belong. We can't say shit because of slander laws. Maybe you should ask *him* what I'm talking about."

Lakota withdrew his blade and tucked it back in the sheath on his belt.

Crow flicked his ashes into the ashtray. "A pack of rogues spotted a two-faced wolf at the crime scene yesterday. They lost a couple of men, and the pack is looking for retribution from the Council. Won't be easy since they're not an official pack, but you better watch your ass, Tonto. You don't run the show around here. You break our laws, and you've got to suffer the consequences like everybody else."

Lakota remained quiet. He was certain the pack Crow was referring to was the one they'd tangled with the day before. Those bastards were probably spreading lies about what had really happened. Lakota and Tak had the right to defend themselves since they'd all been on unclaimed land. But Lakota didn't acknowledge a thing. Gossip was already rampant, and admitting that he and Tak had been hanging around the crime scene would only fuel the fire.

Crow took one last drag off his cigarette and snuffed it out in the ashtray. "Better watch out who you trust, or else that girl of yours might end up being the next sacrificial lamb." He spread his arms over the back of his seat. "*Baaaa.*"

Incensed, Lakota launched out of his seat and stalked out. Crow continued laughing and bleating like a goat. This town was so backward that it made Lakota want to quit the assignment. After spending years traveling from city to city and busting criminals—sometimes slave-trading rings and other times murderers—he'd saved up a lot of cash and gained experience handling any situation. But part of him was ready to settle down. He wasn't sure how much more of it he could take before it made him a colder man.

Lakota hopped in his truck and sped off, leaving a cloud of dust behind him. As asinine as some of the locals were,

Crow might be on to something. *What if it* was *Tak?* The best criminals had gregarious personalities and kept close friendships to throw off suspicion. Lakota remembered research he'd done on psychopaths and sociopaths. They shared similar traits except that psychopaths were often charming and the last people suspected of wrongdoing. What made Tak even more dangerous was that he was an alpha, and by nature, Shifters often felt compelled to submit to an alpha. It wouldn't take much for any of those young girls to comply with his commands had he led them away.

Like the Pied Piper. Wasn't that the name Tak used to describe himself? Lakota recalled Tak's words: "She has to trust you before you decide to pounce."

When Lakota finally reached Shikoba's house, he slammed the truck door and went inside. "Where's Tak?"

A young woman pointed at the kitchen.

Lakota entered the kitchen and saw Tak standing between the counter and the long kitchen island. He had a folded piece of flatbread in his hand.

"Hey, brother," he said, chewing off a piece. "You want some? You're going to need your energy."

Lakota flattened his palms on the island, fingers splayed. "We need to talk."

Tak's eyebrows drew together. After finishing his bite, he pulled out a plate and set his bread on top of it. "What's crawled up your trousers this morning?"

"Were you home all night when Koi was murdered?"

Tak swaggered to the island and mirrored Lakota's position. "Is there something you want to ask me?"

"Can someone vouch for your whereabouts the whole night? That's all I want to know. There's talk in town, and your name was mentioned. Witnesses spotted you that night on someone else's territory."

"They must have seen a ghost."

"What about the murder before that? You were supposed to go to the bar with me that night, and you didn't show up."

"I *told* you I was busy."

"I asked around, Tak. No one had seen you for hours. Kaota had gone up to your room to see if you wanted to go hunting in the morning, and you weren't there."

"Why didn't you mention that?"

Lakota folded his arms. "Didn't seem worth mentioning at the time. You're the last person I would ever suspect of doing this, but if I find out you're involved, I'll have no choice but to go to your father."

Tak's lips thinned. "You have some nerve walking into our home like you own this place and threatening me. Do you have any idea what'll happen if one of us is arrested for these crimes? They'll take our land. It will ruin my father. You're still an outsider, *Sky Hunter*. Don't forget that."

"All you have to do is give me an answer. That's all I need so we can be square. Do you think I want to stand here and accuse my friend of murder? The truth is going to come out one way or the other."

Tak straightened up, his expression stoic. "Brothers look out for each other. Do you think I would let people sully *your* good name—take their word over yours?"

"Are you giving me your word that you had nothing to do with the murders?"

"Why would I kill a woman? Have you forgotten my cousin was slaughtered?"

Lakota wanted to believe him, but Tak was lying about something. He could smell it. "Then *where* were you?"

Waving his hand, Tak walked away. "You're a ghost to me. I don't see you anymore." Before Lakota could press the matter further, Tak left the room.

"*Shit.*" Lakota gripped the edge of the counter and contained his urge to kick something.

He knew better than to form real friendships while on the

job. It made a person biased. But it had still killed him to stand there and accuse Tak of something so heinous. He needed to take a step back in order to conduct his investigation with integrity and honesty. It went beyond friendship or loyalty.

Lives were at stake.

When someone brushed against his back, he jolted forward and spun around. His heart pounded against his chest as he stared down at Melody, who was wearing a wreath of wildflowers around her head. The little white flowers somehow suited the color of her hair and the shade of green in her eyes.

"What are you still doing here? What's with that?" he asked, pointing at her crown.

She lightly touched it and gave him a sheepish grin. "It's for a wedding."

Lakota cocked his head to the side. "Whose?"

She centered her gaze on his, the amusement gone. "Ours."

CHAPTER 16

"D ON'T BE MAD," I SAID, doing my best to placate Lakota.

"Mad?" He glared down at me, eyes volcanic. "Why would I be mad? I'm only going to be mated against my will."

I sighed. "Don't be a drama queen. Come sit down so we can talk."

We approached a round table by the back window and pulled out the chairs.

Lakota moved a vase of flowers aside and rested his forearms on the table. "Explain."

I wasn't sure if there was an easy way to lay it out so that he'd understand. "Look, it's not as bad as it sounds. Shikoba lied to a Councilman so he wouldn't get suspicious about my being here. Lying to the Council is a major offense, and you know that. They showed up unexpectedly, and I was standing around in my nightshirt. Not exactly the behavior of a woman here on business. You get the picture. You're somewhat of an outsider, so the Council bought it and dropped the matter. The thing is, Shikoba's also afraid that his people will lose trust in him if he lies so easily, so he's taking this more seriously than I first thought. After a long talk, we reached an agreement."

"Oh, this sounds good. I leave you alone for five minutes, and we're getting mated."

"We both get something out of this mating ceremony. Shikoba won't look like a liar to the Council or his tribe, and to show his appreciation, he's going to cut a deal with Hope and me. He thinks if I'm mated to someone with Native blood, then he'll have more reason to trust me. Look, the wedding doesn't mean a thing. It's not legal in the eyes of *my* Council since they won't be present or officiating. Tribal laws don't apply to us. Oh, Lakota. This would be *huge* for our business! We talked numbers, and he offered to accept less than what I was willing to pay. Less!"

Lakota shook his head. "I'm not agreeing to this."

My heart sank. I'd known when talking with Shikoba that the offer wasn't firm unless Lakota agreed. "You have to!"

"No, Melody. I don't. You can't play with people's lives like this."

I had to make Lakota understand what everyone stood to gain. "It won't count. It's not a real mating, and we can go about our lives like normal when we leave this place. Shikoba will never find out. It's not like he's going to pop in for a visit, and if he asks how you're doing, I can answer honestly since we'll still keep in touch. Do it for Hope. This would mean so much to her. She doesn't have to know how we closed the deal. This can be our secret." I took off my crown of flowers and set it on the table. "No one ever has to know, and like I said, it won't be legal. What do we have to lose? We're just playing dress-up."

He rubbed his face with his hands, mumbling something unintelligible.

I brushed my finger against a tiny petal on the crown. "This would be a good way to prove your loyalty to Shikoba. We'll go our separate ways in the morning."

"I can't leave, Mel. Not until this case has ended. Besides, how's it going to look if you take off without me?"

I sat back in the chair. "I took care of that. I told him I have to go home and open the store. He also thinks I need time to break this to friends and family, but what he doesn't know won't hurt him. Since this isn't exactly an ordinary negotiation, he doesn't have any say in when we move in together. The ceremony itself is the only thing that's part of our agreement. If he asks, just tell him you have to wrap up some business here or sell your place."

Lakota tilted his head to the side. "I'm staying in a cheap apartment, and as far as they're concerned, I don't work."

I nudged his foot with mine. "Then how are you paying for your apartment? They're not dumb. They know you've got money coming in somehow. Make up a story that you're doing something on the side. That's not exactly a lie. Our agreement had nothing to do with us moving in together."

Lakota snorted. "Just mating for life."

Twirling my hair around my finger, I said, "He thinks it'll be good fortune for his people if he has a mating ceremony just after a burial. The circle of life or something like that."

"Why didn't he ask me himself?"

"You weren't here." I batted my eyelashes. "Maybe he knows you'll do the right thing. Save him from shame and all that."

Lakota groaned as he sat back. "This is worse than the time you made me pretend I was blind."

"It was the only way that cop was going to let a thirteen-year-old off the hook for driving a car."

"I knew I shouldn't have let you behind the wheel, Speedy Gonzales."

Cops in the country sometimes went easy on kids doing dumb things, and that summer Lakota was visiting his family in his new car. Somehow I'd talked him into letting me take it for a spin. My pack had no problem with me driving on the property, but I was a daredevil and wanted to sail down the open road. So when Lakota stopped by to take me over to spend the night with Hope, I convinced him I was an excellent driver. And I was.

Until I reached sixty miles per hour.

I told the cop that Lakota was blind and his grandma had

just had a heart attack and we were on our way home from the hospital.

Lakota sighed. "I'll talk to Shikoba. Maybe there's another way you can make a deal with him that doesn't involve a mating ritual."

I'd already tried everything, but I didn't bother mentioning it. If Lakota could swing a better offer, I would happily take it. "Just don't do anything to jeopardize the deal I have with him. Okay? My clothes are only half the business. If we could secure Shikoba as our supplier, our customers would be lined up out the door."

"Fine."

"What does 'fine' mean?"

He sat forward and rested his arms on the table again. "It means I won't jeopardize your deal."

I felt the excitement bubbling. "So if you can't come up with another deal, does that mean you'll go through with the whole mating thing?"

"Yeah, Mel. I'll be your wife, because clearly you're the one wearing the pants in this relationship."

I sprang out of my chair and hugged him from across the table. "Thank you! Thank you!"

A few giggles erupted from the doorway, and we both glanced at two women who had empty glasses in their hands. They set them on the edge of the counter instead of putting them up and ushered each other out, peering at us with amusement.

I let go of Lakota and slithered back into my chair.

He rubbed his mouth with one hand and reached out with the other. His fingers brushed over my knuckles, and a tender moment passed between us. "Are you okay about everything?"

"Everything" meaning the best night of my life. Yeah, I was pretty good about reading between the lines. "Are *you*?"

His thumb circled over one of my knuckles, and neither of us answered. Maybe the question was more complicated than that, and a simple yes or no wouldn't suffice.